ESCAPE

Alex leapt forward, diving into the next slope. At the same time, there was a sudden chatter, a series of distant cracks, and the snow flew up all around him. Grief's men had machine guns built into their snowmobiles! Alex yelled as he swooped down the mountainside, barely able to control the sheet of metal under his feet. The makeshift binding was tearing at his ankles. The whole thing was vibrating crazily. He couldn't see. He could only hang on, trying to keep his balance, hoping that the way ahead was clear.

He had to get off the mountainside. Otherwise he would be shot or run over. Or both.

"Readers will cheer for Alex Rider!"

—*Publishers Weekly*

"Plenty of slam-bang action, spying and high-tech gadgets. . . . A nonstop thriller."   —*Booklist*

THE ALEX RIDER ADVENTURES

POINT BLANK

POINT BLANK

AN ALEX RIDER ADVENTURE

ANTHONY HOROWITZ

speak

An Imprint of Penguin Group (USA) Inc.

To W.S. and N.

SPEAK

Published by Penguin Group

Penguin Group (USA) Inc.,

345 Hudson Street, New York, New York 10014, U.S.A.

Penguin Books Ltd, 80 Strand, London WC2R ORL, England

Penguin Books Australia Ltd, 250 Camberwell Road,

Camberwell, Victoria 3124, Australia

Penguin Books Canada Ltd, 10 Alcorn Avenue, Toronto, Ontario, Canada M4V 3B2

Penguin Books (N.Z.) Ltd, 182-190 Wairau Road, Auckland 10, New Zealand

First published in the United States of America by Philomel Books,
a division of Penguin Putnam Books for Young Readers, 2002
Published in Great Britain by Walker Books Ltd., London
Published by Speak, an imprint of Penguin Group (USA) Inc., 2004

1 3 5 7 9 10 8 6 4 2

Copyright © Anthony Horowitz, 2001

THE LIBRARY OF CONGRESS HAS CATALOGED THE PHILOMEL EDITION AS FOLLOWS:
Horowitz, Anthony, 1955–
Point Blank: an Alex Rider adventure / Anthony Horowitz.—1st American ed.
p.   cm. Sequel to: Stormbreaker
Summary: Fourteen-year-old Alex Rider continues his work as a spy for the
British MI6, investigating an exclusive school for boys in the French Alps.
[1. Spies—Fiction. 2. Cloning—Fiction. 3. Schools—Fiction. 4. Orphans—Fiction.]
I. Title. PZ7.H7875 Po 2002 [Fic]—dc21 2001033926
ISBN 0-399-23621-X

Speak ISBN 0-14-240164-1

Printed in the United States of America

CONTENTS

1
GOING DOWN

MICHAEL J. ROSCOE was a careful man.

The car that drove him to work at quarter past seven each morning was a custom-made Mercedes with reinforced steel plates and bulletproof windows. His driver, a retired FBI agent, carried a Beretta subcompact automatic pistol and knew how to use it. There were just five steps from the point where the car stopped to the entrance of Roscoe Tower on New York's Fifth Avenue, but closed-circuit television cameras followed him every inch of the way. Once the automatic doors had slid shut behind him, a uniformed guard—also armed—watched as he crossed the foyer and entered his own private elevator.

The elevator had white marble walls, a blue carpet, a silver handrail, and no buttons. Roscoe pressed his hand against a small glass panel. A sensor read his fingerprints, verified them, and activated the elevator. The doors slid shut and the elevator rose to the sixtieth floor without stopping. Nobody else ever used it. Nor did it ever stop at any of the other floors in the building. At the same time it was traveling up, the receptionist in the lobby was on the telephone, letting his staff know that Mr. Roscoe was on his way.

Everyone who worked in Roscoe's private office had been handpicked and thoroughly vetted. It was impossible to see him without an appointment. Getting an appointment could take three months.

When you're rich, you have to be careful. There are cranks, kidnappers, terrorists—the desperate and the dispossessed. Michael J. Roscoe was the chairman of Roscoe Electronics and the ninth or tenth richest man in the world—and he was very careful indeed. Ever since his face had appeared on the front cover of *Time* magazine ("The Electronics King"), he knew that he had become a visible target. When in public he walked quickly, with his head bent. His glasses had been chosen to hide as much as possible of his round, handsome face. His suits were expensive but anonymous. If he went to the theater or to dinner, he always arrived at the last minute, preferring not to hang around. There were dozens of different security systems in his life, and although they had once annoyed him, he had allowed them to become routine.

But ask any spy or security agent. Routine is the one thing that can get you killed. It tells the enemy where you're going and when you're going to be there. Routine was going to kill Michael J. Roscoe, and this was the day death had chosen to come calling.

Of course, Roscoe had no idea of this as he stepped out of the elevator that opened directly into his private office, a huge room occupying the corner of the building with floor-to-ceiling windows giving views in two directions: Fifth Avenue to the east, Central Park just a few blocks north. The two remaining walls contained a door, a low bookshelf, and a single oil painting—a vase of flowers by Vincent van Gogh.

The black glass surface of his desk was equally uncluttered: a computer, a leather notebook, a telephone, and a framed photograph of a fourteen-year-old boy. As he took off his jacket and sat down, Roscoe found himself looking at the picture of the boy. Blond hair, blue eyes, and freckles. Paul Roscoe looked remarkably like his father had thirty years ago. Michael Roscoe was now fifty-two and beginning to show his age despite his year-round tan. His son was almost as tall as he was. The picture had been taken the summer before, on Long Island. They had spent the day sailing. Then they'd had a barbecue on the beach. It had been one of the few happy days they'd ever spent together.

The door opened and his secretary came in. Helen Bosworth was English. She had left her home and, indeed, her husband to come and work in New York, and still loved every minute of it. She had been working in this office for eleven years, and in all that time she had never forgotten a detail or made a mistake.

"Good morning, Mr. Roscoe," she said.

"Good morning, Helen."

She put a folder on his desk. "The latest figures from Singapore. Costings on the R-15 Organizer. You have lunch with Senator Andrews at half past twelve. I've booked The Ivy."

"Did you remember to call London?" Roscoe asked.

Helen Bosworth blinked. She never forgot anything, so why had he asked? "I spoke to Alan Blunt's office yesterday afternoon," she said. Afternoon in New York would have been evening in London. "Mr. Blunt was not available, but I've arranged a person-to-person call with you this afternoon. We can have it patched through to your car."

"Thank you, Helen."

"Shall I have your coffee sent in to you?"

"No, thank you, Helen. I won't have coffee today."

Helen Bosworth left the room, seriously alarmed. No coffee? What next? Mr. Roscoe had begun his day with a double espresso for as long as she had known him. Could it be that he was ill? He certainly hadn't been himself recently—not since Paul had returned home from that school in the South of France. And this phone call to Alan Blunt in London! Nobody had ever told her who he was, but she had seen his name once in a file. He had something to do with military intelligence. MI6. What was Mr. Roscoe doing, talking to a spy?

Helen Bosworth returned to her office and soothed her nerves, not with coffee—she couldn't stand the stuff—but with a refreshing cup of English Breakfast tea. Something very strange was going on, and she didn't like it. She didn't like it at all.

Meanwhile, sixty floors below, a man had walked into the lobby area wearing gray overalls with an ID badge attached to his chest. The badge identified him as Sam Green, maintenance engineer with X-Press

Elevators Inc. He was carrying a briefcase in one hand and a large silver toolbox in the other. He set them both down in front of the reception desk.

Sam Green was not his real name. His hair—black and a little greasy—was fake, as were his glasses, mustache, and uneven teeth. He looked fifty years old, but he was actually closer to thirty. Nobody knew the man's real name, but in the business that he was in, a name was the last thing he could afford. He was known merely as "The Gentleman," and he was one of the highest-paid and most successful contract killers in the world. He had been given his nickname because he always sent flowers to the families of his victims.

The lobby guard glanced at him.

"I'm here for the elevator," he said. He spoke with a Bronx accent even though he had never spent more than a week there in his life.

"What about it?" the guard asked. "You people were here last week."

"Yeah. Sure. We found a defective cable on elevator twelve. It had to be replaced, but we didn't have the parts. So they sent me back." The Gentleman fished in his pocket and pulled out a crumpled sheet of paper. "You want to call the head office? I've got my orders here."

If the guard had called X-Press Elevators Inc., he would have discovered that they did indeed employ a Sam Green—although he hadn't shown up for work in two days. This was because the real Sam Green was at the bottom of the Hudson River with a knife in his back and a twenty-pound block of concrete attached to his foot. But the guard didn't make the call. The Gentleman had guessed he wouldn't bother. After all, the elevators were always breaking down. There were engineers in and out all the time. What difference would one more make?

The guard jerked a thumb. "Go ahead," he said.

The Gentleman put away the letter, picked up his cases, and went over to the elevators. There were a dozen servicing the skyscraper, plus a thirteenth for Michael J. Roscoe. Elevator number twelve was at the end. As he went in, a delivery boy with a parcel tried to follow. "Sorry," The Gentleman said. "Closed for maintenance." The doors slid shut. He was on his own. He pressed the button for the sixty-first floor.

He had been given this job only a week before. He'd had to work fast, killing the real maintenance

engineer, taking his identity, learning the layout of
Roscoe Tower, and getting his hands on the sophisticated piece of equipment he had known he would
need. His employers wanted the multimillionaire elim-
inated as quickly as possible. More importantly, it had
to look like an accident. For this, The Gentleman had
demanded—and been paid—one hundred thousand
dollars. The money was to be paid into a bank
account in Switzerland; half now, half on completion.

The elevator door opened again. The sixty-first
floor was used primarily for maintenance. This was
where the water tanks were housed, as well as the
computers that controlled the heat, air-conditioning,
security cameras, and elevators throughout the building. The Gentleman turned off the elevator, using the
manual override key that had once belonged to Sam
Green, then went over to the computers. He knew exactly where they were. In fact, he could have found
them wearing a blindfold. He opened his briefcase.
There were two sections to the case. The lower part
was a laptop computer. The upper lid was fitted with
a number of drills and other tools, each of them
strapped into place.

It took him fifteen minutes to cut his way into the
Roscoe Tower mainframe and connect his own lap-

top to the circuitry inside. Hacking his way past the
Roscoe security systems took a little longer, but at
last it was done. He tapped a command into his key-
board. On the floor below, Michael J. Roscoe's private elevator did something it had never done before.
It rose one extra floor—to level sixty-one. The door,
however, remained closed. The Gentleman did not
need to get in.

Instead, he picked up the briefcase and the silver
toolbox and carried them back into the same elevator
he had taken from the lobby. He turned the override
key and pressed the button for the fifty-ninth floor.
Once again, he deactivated the elevator. Then he
reached up and pushed. The top of the elevator was
a trapdoor that opened outward. He pushed the briefcase and the silver box ahead of him, then pulled himself up and climbed onto the roof of the elevator. He
was now standing inside the main shaft of Roscoe
Tower. He was surrounded on four sides by girders
and pipes blackened with oil and dirt. Thick steel ca-
bles hung down, some of them humming as they carried their loads. Looking down, he could see a
seemingly endless square tunnel illuminated only by
the chinks of light from the doors that slid open and
shut again as the other elevators arrived at various

floors. Somehow the breeze had made its way in from
the street, spinning dust that stung his eyes. Next to
him was a set of elevator doors that, had he opened
them, would have led him straight into Roscoe's office. Above these, over his head and a few yards to the
right, was the underbelly of Roscoe's private elevator.

The toolbox was next to him, on the roof of the elevator. Carefully, he opened it. The sides of the case
were lined with thick sponge. Inside, in the specially
molded space, was what looked like a complicated
film projector, silver and concave with a thick glass
lens. He took it out, then glanced at his watch. Eight
thirty-five A.M. It would take him an hour to connect
the device to the bottom of Roscoe's elevator, and a
little more to ensure that it was working. He had
plenty of time.

Smiling to himself, The Gentleman took out a
power screwdriver and began to work.

At twelve o'clock, Helen Bosworth called on the telephone. "Your car is here, Mr. Roscoe."

"Thank you, Helen."

Roscoe hadn't done much that morning. He had
been aware that only half his mind was on his work.

Once again, he glanced at the photograph on his desk. Paul. How could things have gone so wrong between a father and a son? And what could have happened in the last few months to make them so much worse?

He stood up, put his jacket on, and walked across his office, on his way to lunch with Senator Andrews. He often had lunch with politicians. They wanted either his money, his ideas—or him. Anyone as rich as Roscoe made for a powerful friend, and politicians need all the friends they can get.

He pressed the elevator button, and the doors slid open. He took one step forward.

The last thing Michael J. Roscoe saw in his life was the inside of his elevator with its white marble walls, blue carpet, and silver handrail. His right foot, wearing a black leather shoe that was handmade for him by a small shop in Rome, traveled down to the carpet and kept going—right through it. The rest of his body followed, tilting into the elevator and then through it. And then he was falling sixty floors to his death.

He was so surprised by what had happened, so totally unable to understand what *had* happened, that he didn't even cry out. He simply fell into the blackness of the elevator shaft, bounced twice off the walls, then crashed into the solid concrete of the basement, five hundred yards below.

The elevator remained where it was. It looked solid but, in fact, it wasn't there at all. What Roscoe had stepped into was a hologram, an image being projected into the empty space of the elevator shaft where the real elevator should have been. The Gentleman had programmed the door to open when Roscoe pressed the call button, and had quietly watched him step into oblivion. If the multimillionaire had managed to look up for a moment, he would have seen the silver hologram projector, beaming the image, a few yards above him. But a man getting into an elevator on his way to lunch does not look up. The Gentleman had known this. And he was never wrong.

At 12:35, the chauffeur called up to say that Mr. Roscoe hadn't arrived at the car. Ten minutes later, Helen Bosworth alerted security, who began to search around the foyer of the building. At one o'clock, they called the restaurant. The senator was there, waiting for his lunch guest. But Roscoe hadn't shown up.

In fact, his body wasn't discovered until the next day, by which time the multimillionaire's disappearance had become the lead story on the news. A bizarre accident—that's what it looked like. Nobody could work out what had happened. Because by that time, of course, The Gentleman had reprogrammed the computer, removed the projector, and left everything as it should have been before quietly leaving the building.

Two days later, a man who looked nothing like a maintenance engineer walked into JFK International Airport. He was about to board a flight for Switzerland. But first, he visited a flower shop and ordered a dozen black tulips to be sent to a certain address. The man paid with cash. He didn't leave a name.

2
BLUE SHADOW

THE WORST TIME TO FEEL alone is when you're in a crowd. Alex Rider was walking across the school yard, surrounded by hundreds of boys and girls his own age. They were all heading in the same direction, all wearing the same blue and gray uniform, all of them thinking probably much the same thoughts. The last lesson of the day had just ended. Homework, supper, and television would fill the remaining hours until bed. Another school day. So why did he feel so out of it, as if he were watching the last weeks of the spring term from the other side of a giant glass screen?

Alex jerked his backpack over one shoulder and continued toward the bike shed. The bag was heavy. As usual, it contained double homework . . . French and history. He had missed three weeks of school and was working hard to catch up. His teachers had not been sympathetic. Nobody had said as much, but when he had finally returned with a doctor's letter ("a bad dose of flu with complications") they had nodded and smiled and secretly thought him a little bit pampered and spoiled. On the other hand, they had to make allowances. They all knew that Alex had no parents, that he had been living with an uncle who had died in some sort of car accident. But even so. Three weeks in bed! Even his closest friends had to admit that was a bit much.

And he couldn't tell them the truth. He wasn't allowed to tell anyone what had really happened. That was the hell of it.

Alex looked around him at the children streaming through the school gates, some dribbling soccer balls, some on their cell phones. He looked at the teachers, curling themselves into their secondhand cars. At first, he had thought the whole school had somehow changed while he was away. But he knew now that what had happened was worse. Everything was the same. He was the one who had changed.

Alex was fourteen years old, an ordinary schoolboy in an ordinary West London school. Or he had been. Three weeks before, he had discovered that his uncle was a secret agent, working for MI6. The uncle—Ian Rider—had been murdered, and MI6 had

forced Alex to take his place. They had given him a
crash course in Special Air Service survival techniques
and sent him on a lunatic mission on the South Coast.
He had been chased, shot at, and almost killed. And
at the end of it he had been packed off and sent back
to school as if nothing had happened. But first they
had made him sign the Official Secrets Act. Alex
smiled at the memory of it. He didn't need to sign
anything. Who would have believed him anyway?

But it was the secrecy that was getting to him
now. Whenever anyone asked him what he had been
doing in the weeks he had been away, he had been
forced to tell them that he had been in bed, reading,
slouching around the house, whatever. Alex didn't
want to boast about what he'd done, but he hated
having to deceive his friends. It made him angry.
MI6 hadn't just put him in danger. They'd locked
his whole life in a filing cabinet and thrown away the
key.

He had reached the bike shed. Somebody muttered a "good-bye" in his direction and he nodded,
then reached up to brush away the single strand of
fair hair that had fallen over his eye. Sometimes he
wished that the whole business with MI6 had never
happened. But at the same time—he had to admit

it—part of him wanted it all to happen again. Sometimes he felt that he no longer belonged in the safe, comfortable world of Brookland Comprehensive. Too much had changed. And at the end of the day, anything was better than double homework.

He lifted his bike out of the shed, unlocked it, pulled the backpack over his shoulders, and prepared to ride away. That was when he saw the beaten-up white car. Back outside the school gates for the second time that week.

Everyone knew about the man in the white car.

He was in his twenties, bald-headed with two broken stumps where his front teeth should have been and five metal studs in his ear. He didn't advertise his name. When people talked about him, they called him Skoda, after the make of his car. But some said that his name was Jake and that he had once been to Brookland. If so, he had come back like an unwelcome ghost; here one minute, vanishing the next . . . somehow always a few seconds ahead of any passing police car or overly inquisitive teacher.

Skoda sold drugs. He sold soft drugs, like pot and cigarettes, to the younger kids, and harder stuff to any of the older ones stupid enough to buy it. It seemed incredible to Alex that Skoda could get away with it so easily, dealing his little packets in broad daylight. But of course, there was a code of honor in the school. No one turned anyone in to the police, not even a rat like Skoda. And there was always the fear that if Skoda went down, some of the people he supplied—friends, classmates—might go with him.

Drugs had never been a huge problem at Brookland, but recently that had begun to change. A clutch of seventeen-year-olds had started buying Skoda's goods, and like a stone dropped into a pool, the ripples had rapidly spread. There had been a spate of thefts, as well as one or two nasty bullying incidents—younger children being forced to bring in money for older ones. The stuff Skoda was selling seemed to get more expensive the more you bought of it, and it hadn't been cheap at the start.

Alex watched as a heavy-shouldered boy with dark eyes and serious acne lumbered over to the car, paused by the open window, and then continued on his way. He felt a sudden spurt of pure loathing. The boy's name was Colin, and a year before, he had been hardworking and popular. These days, he was just avoided. Alex had never thought much about drugs, apart from knowing that he would never take them himself. But he could see that the man in the white car wasn't poisoning just a handful of dumb kids. He was poisoning the whole school.

A policeman on foot patrol appeared, walking toward the gate. A moment later, the white car was gone, black smut bubbling from a faulty exhaust. Alex was on his bike before he knew what he was doing, pedaling fast out of the yard and swerving around the school secretary, who also was on her way home.

"Not too fast, Alex!" she called out, sighing when he ignored her. Miss Bedfordshire had always had a soft spot for Alex without knowing quite why. And she alone in the school had wondered if there hadn't been more to his absence than the doctor's note had suggested.

The white Skoda accelerated down the road, turning left and then right, and Alex thought he was going to lose it. But then it twisted through the maze of back streets that led up to the King's Road and hit the inevitable four o'clock traffic jam, coming to a halt about two hundred yards ahead.

The average speed of traffic in London is—at the start of the twenty-first century—slower than it was in Victorian times. During normal working hours, any bicycle will beat any car on just about any journey at all. And Alex wasn't riding just any bike. He still had his Condor Junior Roadracer, hand-built for him in the workshop that had been open for business on the same street in Holborn for more than fifty years. He'd recently had it upgraded with an integrated brake and gear lever system fitted to the handlebar, and he only had to flick his thumb to feel the bike click up a gear, the lightweight titanium sprockets spinning smoothly beneath him.

He caught up with the car just as it turned the corner and joined the rest of the traffic on the King's Road. He would just have to hope that Skoda was going to stay in the city, but somehow Alex didn't think it likely that he would travel too far. The drug dealer hadn't chosen Brookland Comprehensive as a target simply because he'd been there. It had to be somewhere in his general neighborhood—not too close to home but not too far either.

The lights changed and the white car jerked forward, heading west. Alex pedaled slowly, keeping a few cars behind, just in case Skoda happened to glance in his mirror. They reached the corner known as World's End, and suddenly the road was clear and Alex had to switch gears again and pedal hard to keep up. The car drove on, through Parson's Green and down toward Putney. Alex twisted from one lane to another, cutting in front of a taxi and receiving the blast of a horn as his reward. It was a warm day, and he could feel his French and history homework dragging down his back. How much farther were they going? And what would he do when they got there? Alex was beginning to wonder whether this had been a good idea when the car turned off and he realized they had arrived.

Skoda had pulled into a rough tarmac area, a temporary parking lot next to the River Thames, not far from Putney Bridge. Alex stayed on the bridge, allowing the traffic to roll past, and watched as the dealer got out of his car and began to walk. The area was being redeveloped, another block of prestigious apartments rising up to bruise the London skyline. Right now the building was no more than an ugly skeleton of steel girders and prefabricated concrete slabs. It was surrounded by a swarm of men in hard hats. There were bulldozers, cement mixers, and, towering above them all, a huge, canary yellow crane. A sign read: RIVERVIEW HOUSE. And below it: ALL VISITORS REPORT TO THE SITE OFFICE.

Alex wondered if Skoda had some sort of business

on the site. He seemed to be heading for the entrance. But then he turned off. Alex watched him, increasingly puzzled.

The building site was wedged in between the bridge and a cluster of modern buildings. There was a pub, then what looked like a brand-new conference center, and finally a police station with a parking lot half filled with official cars. But right next to the building site, sticking out into the river, was a wooden jetty with two cabin cruisers and an old iron barge quietly rusting in the murky water. Alex hadn't noticed the jetty at first, but Skoda walked straight onto it, then climbed onto the barge. He found a door, opened it, and disappeared inside. Was this where he lived? It was already growing dark, and somehow Alex doubted he was about to set off on a pleasure cruise down the River Thames.

He got back on his bike and cycled slowly to the end of the bridge, and then down toward the parking lot. He left the bike and his backpack out of sight and continued on foot, moving more slowly as he approached the jetty. He wasn't afraid of being caught. This was a public place, and even if Skoda did reappear, there would be nothing he could do. But he was curious. Just what was the dealer doing on board a barge? It seemed a bizarre place to have stopped. Alex still wasn't sure what he was going to do, but he wanted to have a look inside. Then he would decide.

The wooden jetty creaked under his feet as he stepped onto it. The barge was called *Blue Shadow,* but there was little blue left in the flaking paint, the rusty ironwork, and the dirty, oil-covered decks. The barge was about thirty yards long and very square with a single cabin in the center. It was lying low in the water, and Alex guessed that most of the living quarters would be underneath. He knelt down on the jetty and pretended to tie his shoelaces, hoping to look through the narrow, slanting windows. But all the curtains were drawn. What now?

The barge was moored on one side of the jetty. The two cabin cruisers were side by side on the other. Skoda wanted privacy—but he must also need light, and there would be no need to draw the curtains on the far side, with nothing there but the river. The only trouble was that to look in the other windows, Alex would have to climb onto the barge itself. He considered briefly. It had to be worth the risk. He was near enough to the building site. Nobody was going to try to hurt him in broad daylight.

He placed one foot on the deck, then slowly

transferred his weight onto it. He was afraid that moving the barge would give him away. Sure enough, the barge dipped under his weight, but Alex had chosen his moment well. A police launch was sailing past, heading up the river and back into town. The barge bobbed naturally in its wake, and by the time it settled, Alex was on board, crouching next to the cabin door.

Now he could hear music coming from inside. The heavy beat of a rock band. He didn't want to do it, but he knew there was only one way to look in. He tried to find an area of the deck that wasn't too covered in oil, then lay flat on his stomach. Clinging on to the handrail, he lowered his head and shoulders over the side of the barge and shifted himself forward so that he was hanging almost upside down over the water.

He was right. The curtains on this side of the barge were open. Looking through the dirty glass of the window, he could see two men. Skoda was sitting on a bunk, smoking a cigarette. There was a second man, blond-haired and ugly, with twisted lips and three days' stubble, wearing a torn sweatshirt and jeans, making a cup of coffee at a small stove. The music was coming from a boom box perched on a shelf. Alex looked around the cabin. Besides two bunks and the miniature kitchen, the barge offered no living accommodations at all. Instead, it had been converted for another purpose. Skoda and his friend had turned it into a floating laboratory.

There were two metal work surfaces, a sink, and a pair of electric scales. Everywhere there were test tubes and Bunsen burners, flasks, glass pipes, and measuring spoons. The whole place was filthy—obviously neither of the two men cared about hygiene— but Alex knew that he was looking into the heart of their operation. This was where they prepared the drugs they sold: cut them down, weighed them, and packaged them for delivery to local schools. It was an insane idea to put a drug factory on a boat, almost in the middle of London, and only a stone's throw away from a police station. But at the same time, it was a clever one. Who would have looked for it here?

The blond-haired man suddenly turned around, and Alex hooked his body up and slithered backward onto the deck. For a moment he was dizzy. Hanging upside down had made the blood drain into his head. He took a couple of breaths, trying to collect his thoughts. It would be easy enough to walk over to the police station and tell the officer in charge what he had seen. The police could take over from there.

But something inside Alex rejected the idea. Maybe he would have done that a few months before: let someone else take care of it. But he hadn't cycled all this way just to call the police. He thought back to his first sighting of the white car outside the school gates. He remembered his friend Colin shuffling over to it and felt once again a brief blaze of anger. This was something he wanted to do himself.

But what could he do? If the barge had been equipped with a plug, Alex would have pulled it out and sunk the entire thing. But of course it wasn't as easy as that. The barge was tied to the jetty by two thick ropes. He could untie them, but that wouldn't help either. The barge would drift away, but this was Putney. There were no whirlpools or waterfalls. Skoda could simply turn on the engine and cruise back again.

Alex looked around him. On the building site, the day's work was coming to an end. Some of the men were already leaving, and as he watched, he saw a trapdoor open about a hundred and fifty yards above him and a stocky man begin the long climb down from the top of the crane. Alex closed his eyes. A whole series of images suddenly flashed into his mind, like different sections of a jigsaw puzzle.

The barge. The building site. The police station.

The crane with its big hook, dangling underneath the jib.

And the Blackpool amusement park. He'd gone there once with his housekeeper, Jack Starbright, and had watched as she won a teddy bear, hooking it out of a glass case and carrying it over to a chute.

Could it be done? Alex looked again, working out the angles. Yes. It probably could.

He stood up and crept back across the deck to the door that Skoda had entered. A length of wire was lying to one side, and he picked it up, then wound it several times around the handle of the door. He looped the wire over a hook in the wall and pulled it tight. The door was effectively locked. There was a second door at the back of the boat. Alex secured this one with his own bicycle padlock. As far as he could see, the windows were too narrow to crawl through. There was no other way in or out.

He crept off the barge and back onto the jetty. Then he untied it, leaving the thick rope loosely curled up beside the metal pegs—the stanchions—that had secured it. The river was still. It would be a while before the barge drifted away.

He straightened up. Satisfied with his work so far, he began to run.

3

HOOKED

THE ENTRANCE TO THE BUILDING site was crowded with construction workers preparing to go home. Alex was reminded of Brookland an hour earlier. Nothing really changed when you got older—except that maybe you weren't given homework. The men and women drifting out of the site were tired, in a hurry to be away. That was probably why none of them tried to stop Alex as he slipped in among them, walking purposefully as if he knew where he was going, as if he had every right to be there.

But the shift wasn't completely finished yet. Other workers were still carrying tools, stowing away machinery, packing up for the night. They all wore protective headgear, and seeing a pile of plastic helmets, Alex snatched one up and put it on. The great sweep of the block of apartments that was being built loomed up ahead of him. To pass through it, he was forced into a narrow corridor between two scaffolding towers. Suddenly a heavy-set man in white overalls stepped in front of him, blocking his way.

"Where are you going?" he demanded.

"My dad . . ." Alex gestured vaguely in the direction of another worker and kept walking. The trick worked. The man didn't challenge him again.

He headed toward the crane. It stood in the open, the high priest of construction. Alex hadn't realized how very tall it was until he had reached it. The supporting tower was bolted into a massive block of concrete. It was very narrow—once he squeezed through the iron girders, he could reach out and touch all four sides. A ladder ran straight up the center. Without stopping to think, Alex began to climb.

It's only a ladder, he told himself. You've climbed ladders before. You've got nothing to worry about. But this was a ladder with three hundred rungs. If Alex let go or slipped, there would be nothing to stop him from falling to his death. There were rest platforms at intervals, but Alex didn't dare stop to catch his breath. Somebody might look up and see him. And there was always a chance that the barge, loose from its moorings, might begin to drift. Alex knew he had to hurry.

After two hundred and fifty rungs, the tower

narrowed. Alex could see the crane's control cabin directly above him. He looked back down. The men on the building site were suddenly very small and far away. He climbed the last ladder. There was a trapdoor over his head, leading into the cabin. But the trapdoor was locked.

Fortunately, Alex was ready for this. When MI6 had sent him on his first mission, they had given him a number of gadgets—he couldn't exactly call them weapons—to help him out of a tight spot. One of these was a tube marked ZIT-CLEAN, FOR HEALTHIER SKIN. But the cream inside the tube did much more than clean up pimples.

Although Alex had used most of it, he had managed to hold on to the last remnants and often carried the tube with him as a sort of souvenir. He had it in his pocket now. Holding on to the ladder with one hand, he took the tube out with the other. There was very little of the cream left, but Alex knew that a little was all he needed. He opened the tube, squeezed some of the cream onto the lock, and waited. There was a moment's pause, then a hiss and a wisp of smoke. The cream was eating into the metal. The lock sprang open. Alex pushed back the trapdoor and climbed the last few rungs. He was in.

He had to close the trapdoor again to create enough floor space to stand on. He found himself in a square, metal box, about the same size as a sit-in arcade game. There was a pilot's chair with two joysticks—one on each arm—and instead of a screen, a floor-to-ceiling window with a spectacular view of the building site, the river, and the whole of West London. A small computer monitor had been built into one corner, and at knee level, there was a radio transmitter.

The joysticks beside the arms were surprisingly uncomplicated. Each had just six buttons—two green, two black, and two red. There were even helpful diagrams to show what they did. The right hand lifted the hook up and down. The left hand moved it along the jib, closer or farther from the cabin. The left hand also controlled the whole top of the crane, rotating it three hundred and sixty degrees. It couldn't have been much simpler. Even the START button was clearly labeled. A big switch for a big toy.

He turned the switch and felt power surge into the control cabin. The computer lit up with a graphic of a barking dog as the warm-up program spun into life. Alex eased himself into the operator's chair. There were still twenty or thirty men on the site. Looking down between his knees, he saw them moving silently far below. Nobody had noticed that anything was wrong. But still he knew he had to move fast.

He pressed the green button on the right-hand control—green for go—then touched his fingers against the joystick and pushed. Nothing happened! Alex frowned. Maybe it was going to be more complicated than he'd thought. What had he missed? He rested his hands on the joysticks, looking left and right for another control. His right hand moved slightly and suddenly the hook soared up from the ground. It was working!

Unknown to Alex, heat sensors concealed inside the handles of the joysticks had read his body temperature and activated the crane. All modern cranes have the same security system built into them, in case the operator has a heart attack and dies. There can be no accidents. Body heat is needed to make the crane work.

And luckily for him, this crane was a Liebherr 154 EC-H, one of the most modern in the world. The Liebherr is incredibly easy to use, and also remarkably accurate. Even sitting so high above the ground, the operator can pick up a tea bag and drop it into a small china pot. Now Alex pushed sideways with his left hand and gasped as the crane swung around. In front of him he could see the jib stretching out, swinging high over the rooftops of London. The more he pushed, the faster the crane went. The movement couldn't have been smoother. The Liebherr 154 has a fluid coupling between the electric motor and the gears so that it never jolts or shudders. It glides. Alex found a white button under his thumb and pressed it. The movement stopped at once.

He was ready. He would need some beginner's luck, but he was sure he could do it, provided nobody looked up and saw the crane moving. He pushed with his left hand again and this time waited as the jib of the crane swung all the way around past Putney Bridge and over the River Thames. When the jib was pointing directly at the barge, he stopped. Now he maneuvered the cradle with the hook, using his other hand. First he slid it right to the end of the jib. Then he lowered it, quickly to begin with, more slowly as it drew closer to ground level. The hook was solid metal. If he hit the barge, Skoda might hear it, and he would have given himself away. Carefully, now, one inch at a time. Alex licked his lips and, using all his concentration, took careful aim.

The hook crashed onto the deck. Alex cursed. Surely Skoda would have heard it and would even now be grappling with the door. Then he remembered the boom box. With luck, the music would have drowned out the noise. He lifted the hook, at the same time dragging it across the deck toward him. He had seen his target. There was a thick metal stanchion welded into the deck at the near end. If he could just loop the hook around the stanchion, he would have caught his fish. Then he could reel it in.

His first attempt missed the stanchion by more than a foot. Alex forced himself not to panic. He had to do this slowly or he would never do it at all. Working with his left and right hands, balancing one movement against the other, he dragged the hook over the deck and then back toward the stanchion. He would just have to hope that the boom box was still playing and that the sliding metal wasn't making too much noise. He missed the stanchion a second time. This wasn't going to work! No. He could do it. It was the same as the game at the amusement park . . . just bigger. He gritted his teeth and maneuvered the hook a third time. This time he saw it happen. The hook caught hold of the stanchion. He had it!

He looked down. Nobody had noticed anything wrong. Now . . . how do you lift? He pulled with his right hand. The hook tightened. The cable became taut. He actually felt the crane take the weight of the barge. The whole tower tilted forward alarmingly, and Alex almost slid out of his seat. For the first time he wondered whether his plan was actually possible. Could the crane lift the barge out of the water? What was the maximum load? There was a white placard at the end of the crane arm, printed with a measurement—3900KG. Alex made a quick calculation. That was about five tons. Surely the boat couldn't weigh that much. He glanced at the computer screen. One set of digits was changing so rapidly he was unable to read them. They were showing the weight that the crane was taking. What would happen if the boat *was* too heavy? Would the computer initiate an automatic cutoff? Or would the whole thing just fall over?

Alex settled himself in the chair and pulled back, wondering what would happen next.

Inside the boat, Skoda was opening a bottle of gin. He'd had a good day, selling more than a hundred and fifty dollars' worth of merchandise to the kids at his old school. And the best thing was, they'd all be back for more. Soon, he'd sell them the stuff only if they promised to introduce it to their friends. Then the friends would become customers too. It was the easiest market in the world. He'd gotten them hooked. They were his to do with as he liked.

The fair-haired man working with him was named Beckett. The two had met in prison and decided to go into business together when they got out. The boat had been Beckett's idea. There was no real kitchen and no toilet, and it was freezing in winter . . . but it worked. It even amused them to be so close to a police station. Sometimes they enjoyed watching the police cars or boats going past. Of course, the pigs would never think of looking for criminals right on their own doorstep.

Suddenly Beckett swore. "What the . . . ?"

"What is it?" Skoda looked up.

"The cup . . ."

Skoda watched as a cup of coffee, which had been sitting on a shelf, began to move. It slid sideways, then fell off with a clatter, spilling cold coffee on the gray rag that they called a carpet. Skoda was confused. The cup seemed to have moved on its own. Nothing had touched it. He giggled. "How did you do that?" he asked.

"I didn't . . ."

"Then . . ."

The fair-haired man was the first to realize what

was happening—but even he couldn't guess the truth. "We're sinking!" he shouted.

He scrabbled for the door. Now Skoda felt it for himself. The floor was tilting. Test tubes and beakers slid into each other, then crashed to the floor, glass shattering. He swore and followed Beckett—uphill now. With every second that passed, the gradient grew steeper. But the strange thing was that the barge didn't seem to be sinking at all. On the contrary, the front of it seemed to be rising out of the water.

"What's going on?" Skoda yelled.

"The door's jammed!" Beckett had managed to open it an inch, but the wire on the other side was holding it firm. "Check the other door!"

But the second door was now high above them. More bottles rolled off the table and smashed. In the kitchen, dirty plates and mugs slid into each other, pieces flying. With something between a sob and a snarl, Skoda tried to climb up the mountainside that the inside of the boat had become. But it was already too steep. The door was almost over his head. He lost his balance and fell backward, shouting as, one second later, the other man was thrown on top of him. The two of them rolled into the corner, tangled up in each other. Plates, cups, knives, forks, and dozens of pieces of scientific equipment crashed into them. The walls of the barge were grinding with the pressure. A window shattered. A table turned itself into a battering ram and hurled itself at them. Skoda felt a bone snap in his arm and screamed out loud.

The barge was completely vertical, standing in the water at ninety degrees. For a moment it rested where it was. Then it began to rise. . . .

Alex stared at the barge in amazement. The crane was lifting it at half speed—some sort of override had come into action, slowing the operation down—but it wasn't even straining. Alex could feel the power under his palms. Sitting in the cabin with both hands on the joysticks, his feet apart and the jib of the crane jutting out ahead of him, he felt as if he and the crane had become one. He had only to move an inch and the five-ton boat would be brought to him. He could see it, dangling on the hook, spinning slowly. Water was streaming off the bow. It was already clear of the water, rising up about five yards per second. He wondered what it must be like inside.

And then the radio beside his knee hissed into life.

"Crane operator! This is base. What the hell do you think you're doing? Over!" A pause, a burst of static.

Then the metallic voice was back. "Who is in the crane? Who's up there? Will you identify yourself . . ."

There was a microphone snaking toward Alex's chin and he was tempted to say something. But he decided against it. Hearing a teenager's voice would only panic them more.

He looked down between his knees. About a dozen construction workers were closing in on the base of the crane. Others were pointing at the boat, jabbering amongst themselves. No sounds reached the cabin. It was as if Alex were cut off from the real world. He felt very secure. He had no doubt that more workers had already started climbing the ladder and that it would all be over soon, but for the moment he was untouchable. He concentrated on what he was doing. Getting the barge out of the water had been only half his plan. He still had to finish it.

"Crane operator! Lower the hook! We believe there are people inside the boat and you are endangering their lives. Repeat. Lower the hook!"

The barge was almost two hundred feet above the water, swinging on the end of the hook. Alex moved his left hand, turning the crane around so that the boat was dragged in an arc along the river and then over dry land. There was a sudden buzz. The jib came to a halt. Alex pushed the joystick. Nothing happened. He glanced at the computer. The screen had gone blank.

Someone at ground level had come to his senses and done the only sensible thing. He had switched off the power. The crane was dead.

Alex sat where he was, watching the barge swaying in the breeze. He hadn't quite succeeded in what he had set out to do. He had planned to lower the boat—along with its contents—safely into the parking lot by the police station. It would have made a nice surprise for the authorities, he had thought. Instead the boat was now hanging over the conference center that he had seen from Putney Bridge. But at the end of the day, he supposed it didn't make much difference. The result would be the same.

He stretched his arms and relaxed, waiting for the trapdoor to burst open. This wasn't going to be easy to explain.

And then he heard the tearing sound.

The metal stanchion that protruded from the end of the deck had never been designed to carry the entire weight of the barge. It was a miracle that it had lasted as long as it had. As Alex watched, open-mouthed, the stanchion tore itself free. For a few sec-

onds it clung by one edge to the deck. Then the last
metal rivet came loose.

The five-ton barge had been sixty yards above the
ground. Now it began to fall.

In the Putney Riverside Conference Center, the chief
of the Metropolitan Police was addressing a large
crowd of journalists, TV cameramen, civil servants,
and government officials. He was a tall, thin man who
took himself very seriously. His dark blue uniform
was immaculate, with every piece of silver—from the
studs on his epaulettes to his five medals—polished
until it gleamed. This was his big day. He was sharing
the platform with no less a personage than the home
secretary himself. The assistant chief of police was
there as well as seven lower-ranking officers. A slogan
was being projected onto the wall behind him.

WINNING THE WAR AGAINST DRUGS

Silver letters on a blue background. The chief of
police had chosen the colors himself, knowing that
they matched his uniform. He liked the slogan. He
knew it would be in all the major newspapers the next
day—along with, just as important, a photograph of
himself.

"We have overlooked nothing!" he was saying, his

voice echoing around the modern room. He could see the journalists scribbling down his every word. The television cameras were all focused on him. "Thanks to my personal involvement and efforts, we have never been more successful." He smiled at the home secretary, who smiled toothily back. "But we are not resting on our laurels. Oh, no! Any day now we hope to announce another breakthrough."

That was when the barge hit the glass roof of the conference center. There was an explosion. The chief of police just had time to dive for cover as a vast, dripping object plunged down toward him. The home secretary was thrown backward, his glasses flying off his face. His security men froze, helpless. The boat crashed into the space in front of them, between the stage and the audience. The side of the cabin had been torn off, and there was the laboratory, exposed, with the two dealers sprawled together in one corner, staring dazedly at the hundreds of policemen and officials who now surrounded them. A cloud of white powder mushroomed up and then fell onto the dark blue uniform of the police chief, covering him from head to toe. The fire alarms had all gone off. The lights blew out. Then the screaming began.

Meanwhile, the first of the construction workers had made it to the crane cabin and was gazing, astonished, at the fourteen-year-old boy he had found there.

"Do you . . . ?" he stammered. "Do you have any idea what you've just done?"

Alex glanced at the empty hook and at the gaping hole in the roof of the conference center, at the rising smoke and dust. He shrugged apologetically.

"I was just working on the crime figures," he said. "And I think there's been a drop."

4

SEARCH AND REPORT

AT LEAST THEY DIDN'T have far to take him.

Two men brought Alex down from the crane, one above him on the ladder and one below. The police were waiting at the bottom. Watched by the incredulous construction workers, he was marched away from the building site and into the police station just a few doors away. As he passed the conference center, he saw the crowds pouring out. Ambulances had already arrived. The home secretary was being whisked away in a black limousine. For the first time, Alex was seriously worried, wondering if anyone had been killed. He hadn't meant it to end like this.

Once they got to the police station, everything happened in a whirl of slamming doors, blank official faces, whitewashed walls, forms, and phone calls. Alex was asked his name, his age, his address. He saw a police sergeant tapping the details into a computer, but what happened next took him by surprise. The sergeant pressed ENTER and visibly froze. He turned and looked at Alex, then hastily left his seat. When Alex had entered the police station, he had been the center of attention, but suddenly everyone was avoiding his eye. A more senior officer appeared. Words were exchanged. Alex was led down a corridor and put into a cell.

Half an hour later, a female police officer appeared with a tray of food. "Supper," she said.

"What's happening?" Alex asked. The woman smiled nervously, but said nothing. "I left my bike by the bridge," Alex said.

"It's all right. We've got it." She couldn't leave the room fast enough.

Alex ate the food: sausages, toast, a slice of cake. There was a bunk in the room and, behind a screen, a sink and a toilet. He wondered whether anyone was going to come in and talk to him, but nobody did. Eventually he fell asleep.

The next thing he knew, it was seven o'clock in the morning. The door was open and a man he knew all too well was standing in the cell, looking down at him.

"Good morning, Alex," he said.

"Mr. Crawley."

John Crawley looked like a junior bank manager,

and when Alex had first met him, he had indeed been pretending that he worked for a bank. The cheap suit and striped tie could both have come from the Macy's "Boring Businessman" section. In fact, Crawley worked for MI6. Alex wondered if the clothes were a cover or a personal choice.

"You can come with me now," Crawley said. "We're leaving."

"Are you taking me home?" Alex asked. He wondered if anyone had been told where he was.

"No. Not yet."

Alex followed Crawley out of the building. This time there were no police officers in sight. A car with a driver stood waiting outside. Crawley got into the back with Alex.

"Where are we going?" Alex asked.

"You'll see." Crawley opened a copy of the *Daily Telegraph* and began to read. He didn't speak again.

They drove east through the City and toward Liverpool Street. Alex knew at once where he was being taken, and sure enough, the car turned into the entrance of a seventeen-story building near the station and disappeared down a ramp into an underground parking lot. Alex had been here before. The building pretended to be the headquarters of the Royal & General Bank. In fact, this was where the Special Operations division of MI6 was based.

The car stopped. Crawley folded away his paper and got out, ushering Alex ahead of him. There was an elevator in the basement, and the two of them took it to the sixteenth floor.

"This way." Crawley gestured at a door marked 1605. The Gunpowder Plot, Alex thought. It was an absurd thing to flash into his mind, a fragment of the history homework he should have been doing the night before. Guy Fawkes had tried to blow up the Houses of Parliament in the year 1605. Oh well, it looked as if the homework was going to have to wait.

Alex opened the door and went in. Crawley didn't follow. When Alex looked around, the man was already walking away.

"Shut the door, Alex, and come in."

Once again, Alex found himself standing opposite the prim, unsmiling man who ran MI6. Gray suit, gray face, gray life . . . Alan Blunt seemed to belong to an entirely colorless world. He was sitting behind a wooden desk in a large square office that could have belonged to any business anywhere in the world. There was nothing personal in the room, not even a picture on the wall or a photograph on the desk. Even the pigeons pecking on the windowsill outside were gray.

He was not alone. Mrs. Jones, the head of Special Operations, was with him, sitting on a leather chair, wearing a mud-brown jacket and dress, and as always, sucking a peppermint. She looked up at Alex with black, beadlike eyes. She seemed to be more pleased to see him than her boss was. She was the one who had spoken. Blunt had barely registered the fact that Alex had come into the room.

Then Blunt looked up. "I hadn't expected to see you again so soon," he said.

"That's just what I was going to say," Alex replied. There was a single empty chair in the office. He sat down.

Blunt slid a sheet of paper across his desk and examined it briefly. "What on earth were you thinking?" he demanded. "This business with the crane. You've done an enormous amount of damage. You practically destroyed a three-million-dollar conference center. It's a miracle nobody was killed."

"The two men who were in the boat will be in the hospital for months," Mrs. Jones added.

"You could have killed the home secretary!" Blunt continued. "That would have been the last straw. What were you doing?"

"They were drug dealers," Alex said.

"So we've discovered. But the normal procedure would have been to call the police."

"I couldn't find a phone." Alex sighed. "They turned off the crane," he explained. "I was going to put the boat next to the police department. On the doorstep."

Blunt blinked once and waved a hand as if dismissing everything that had happened. "It's just as well that your special status came up on the police computer," he said. "They called us—and we've handled the rest."

"I didn't know I had special status," Alex said.

"Oh, yes, Alex. You're nothing if not special." Blunt gazed at him for a moment. "That's why you're here."

"So you're not going to send me home?"

"No. The fact is, Alex, that we were thinking of contacting you anyway. We need you again."

"You're probably the only person who can do what we have in mind," Mrs. Jones added.

"Wait a minute!" Alex shook his head. "I've still got two weeks of school before Easter. I'm far enough behind as it is. Suppose I'm not interested?"

Mrs. Jones sighed. "We could, of course, return you to the police," she said. "As I understand it, they were very eager to interview you."

"And how is Miss Starbright?" Blunt asked.

Jack Starbright—Alex still didn't know if the name was short for Jackie or for Jacqueline—was the housekeeper who had been looking after Alex since his uncle had died. She was a bright, red-haired American girl who had come to London to study law but had never left. Blunt wasn't interested in her health—Alex knew that. The last time they'd met, he'd made his position clear. So long as Alex did as he was told, he could keep living in his uncle's apartment with Jack. Step out of line and she'd be deported to America.

Alex liked Jack. For ten years, she'd almost been like a big sister to him. He also needed her. He knew that he was too young to live on his own and that once she was out of the picture, the authorities would have custody of him. That would mean some grim institution in the north of England. Blunt had made that clear too.

"Have you told Jack where I am?" he asked.

"Of course. She doesn't seem to like the idea of our . . . employing you. Actually, I must remember to get her to sign the Official Secrets Act. I wouldn't want her talking to the wrong people."

Mrs. Jones took over. "Come on, Alex," she said. "Why pretend you're an ordinary schoolboy anymore?" She was trying to sound more friendly, more like a mother. But even snakes have mothers, Alex thought. "You've already proven yourself once," she went on. "We're just giving you a chance to do it again."

"It'll probably come to nothing," Blunt continued. "It's just something that needs looking into. What we call a search and report."

"Why can't Crawley do it?"

"We need a boy."

Alex fell silent. He looked from Blunt to Mrs. Jones and back again. He knew that neither of them would hesitate for a second before pulling him out of Brookland, taking him away from his friends, and sending him . . . wherever. Anyway, wasn't this what he had been asking for only the day before? Another adventure. Another chance to save the world.

"All right," he said. "What is it this time?"

Blunt nodded at Mrs. Jones, who unwrapped another peppermint and began.

"I wonder if you know anything about a man called Michael J. Roscoe?" she asked.

Alex thought for a moment. "He was that businessman who had an accident in New York." He'd seen the news on TV. "Didn't he fall down an elevator shaft or something?"

"Roscoe Electronics is one of the largest companies in America," Mrs. Jones said. "In fact, it's one of the largest in the world. Computers, videos, DVD players . . . everything from cell phones to washing machines. Roscoe was very rich, very influential—"

"And very clumsy," Alex cut in.

"It certainly seems to have been a very strange and even careless accident," Mrs. Jones agreed. "The elevator somehow malfunctioned. Roscoe didn't look where he was going. He fell into the shaft and died. That's the general opinion. However, we're not so sure."

"Why not?"

"First of all, there are a number of details that don't add up. On the day Roscoe died, a maintenance engineer by the name of Sam Green called at the office building on Fifth Avenue where Roscoe worked. We know it was Green—or someone who looked very much like him—because we've seen him. They have closed-circuit security cameras, and he was filmed going in. He said he'd come to look at a defective cable. But according to the company that employed him, there was no defective cable and he certainly wasn't acting under orders from them."

"Why don't you talk to him?"

"We'd like to. But Green has vanished without a trace. We think he may have been killed. We think someone may have taken his place and somehow set up the accident that killed Roscoe."

Alex shrugged. "I'm sorry. I'm sorry about Mr. Roscoe. But what's it got to do with me?"

"I'm coming to that." Mrs. Jones paused. "The strangest thing of all is that the day before he died, Roscoe telephoned this office. A personal call. He asked to speak to Alan Blunt."

"I met Roscoe at Cambridge University," Blunt said. "That was a long time ago. We became friends."

That surprised Alex. He didn't think of Blunt as the sort of man who had friends. "What did he say?" he asked.

"Unfortunately, I wasn't here to take the call," Blunt replied. "I arranged to speak with him the following day. By that time, it was too late."

"Do you have any idea what he wanted?"

"I spoke to his assistant," Mrs. Jones said. "She wasn't able to tell me very much, but she understood that Roscoe wanted to talk to us about his son. He had a fourteen-year-old son, Paul Roscoe."

A fourteen-year-old son. Alex was beginning to see the way things were going.

"Paul was his only son," Blunt explained. "I'm afraid the two of them had a very difficult relationship. Roscoe divorced a few years ago, and although the boy chose to live with his father, they didn't really get along. There were the usual teenage problems, but of course, when you grow up surrounded by millions of dollars, these problems sometimes get amplified. Paul was doing badly at school. He was playing hooky and spending time with some very undesirable friends. There was an incident with the New York police—nothing serious, and Roscoe managed to hush it up—but still, it upset him. I spoke to Roscoe from time to time. He was worried about Paul and felt the boy was out of control. But there didn't seem to be very much he could do."

"So is that what you want me for?" Alex interrupted. "You want me to meet this boy and talk to him about his father's death?"

"No." Blunt shook his head and handed a file to Mrs. Jones.

She opened it. Alex caught a glimpse of a photograph: a dark-skinned man in military uniform. "Remember what we told you about Roscoe," she said, "because now I want to tell you about another man." She slid the photograph around so that Alex could see it. "This is General Major Viktor Ivanov. Ex-KGB. Until last December he was the head of the Foreign Intelligence Service and probably the second or third most powerful man in Russia after the president. But then something happened to him too. It was a boating accident on the Black Sea. His cruiser exploded . . . nobody knows why."

"Was he a friend of Roscoe's?" Alex asked.

"They probably never met. But we have a department here that constantly monitors world news, and their computers have thrown up a very strange coincidence. Ivanov also had a fourteen-year-old son . . . Dimitry. And one thing is certain. The young Ivanov certainly knew the young Roscoe because they went to the same school."

"Paul and Dimitry . . ." Alex was puzzled. "What was a Russian boy doing at a school in New York?"

"He wasn't in New York." Blunt took over. "As I told you, Roscoe was having trouble with his boy. Trouble at school, trouble at home. So last year he decided to take action. He sent Paul to Europe, to a place in France, a sort of finishing school. Do you know what a finishing school is?"

"I thought it was the sort of place where rich people used to send their daughters," Alex said. "To learn table manners."

"That's the general idea. But this school is for boys only, and not just ordinary boys. The fees are fifteen thousand dollars a term. This is the brochure here. You can have a look." He passed a heavy square booklet to Alex. Written on the cover, gold letters on black, were two words: POINT BLANC. "It's right on the French-Swiss border," he explained. "South of Geneva. Just above Grenoble, in the French Alps. It's pronounced *Point Blanc*. . . ." He spoke the words with a French accent. "Literally, white point. It's a remarkable place. Built as a private home by some lunatic in the nineteenth century. As a matter of fact, that's what it became after he died—a lunatic asylum.

It was taken over by the Germans in the Second World War. They used it as a recreation center for their senior staff. After that, it fell into disrepair until it was bought by the current owner, a man called Grief. Dr. Hugo Grief. He's the principal of the school."

Alex opened the brochure and found himself looking at a color photograph of Point Blanc. Blunt was right. The school was like nothing he had ever seen, something between a German castle and a French chateau, straight out of a Grimms' fairy tale. But what made Alex draw his breath, more than the building itself, was the setting. The school was perched on top of a mountain, with nothing but mountains all around, a great pile of brick and stone surrounded by a snow-covered landscape. It seemed to have no business being there, as if it had been snatched out of an ancient city and accidentally dropped there. No roads led to or from the school. The snow continued all the way to the front gate. But looking again, Alex saw a modern helicopter pad projecting over the battlements. He guessed that it was the only way to get there . . . and to leave.

He turned another page.

Welcome to the Academy at Point Blanc, the

introduction began. It had been printed with the sort
of lettering Alex would expect to find in the menu of
an expensive restaurant. *A unique school that is much
more than a school, created for boys who need more
than the ordinary education system can provide. In our
time, we have been called a school for "problem children," but we do not believe the term applies. There are
problems and there are children. It is our aim to separate the two.*

"There's no need to read all that stuff," Blunt said.
"All you need to know is that the academy takes in
boys who have been expelled from all their other
schools. There are never very many of them there—
just six or seven at a time. And it's unique in other
ways too. For a start, it takes only the sons of the
super-rich."

"At fifteen thousand dollars per term, I'm not surprised," Alex said.

"You'd be surprised just how many parents have
applied to send their sons there," Blunt went on. "But
I suppose you've only got to look at the newspapers
to see how easy it is to go off the rails when you're
born with a silver spoon in your mouth. It doesn't
matter if they're politicians or pop stars, fame and fortune for the parents often bring problems for the chil-

dren . . . and the more successful they are, the more pressure there seems to be. The academy went into business to straighten the young people out, and by all accounts it's been a great success."

"It was established twenty years ago," Mrs. Jones said. "In that time it's had a client list you'd find hard to believe. Of course, they've kept the names confidential. But I can tell you that parents who have sent their children there include an American vice president, a Nobel Prize–winning scientist, and a member of our own royal family."

"As well as Roscoe and this man, Ivanov," Alex said.

"Yes."

Alex shrugged. "So it's a coincidence. Just like you said. Two rich parents with two rich kids at the same school. They're both killed in accidents. Why are you so interested?"

"Because I don't like coincidence," Blunt replied. "In fact, I don't believe in coincidence. Where some people see coincidence, I see conspiracy. That's my job."

And you're welcome to it, Alex thought. What he said was, "Do you really think the school and this man—Grief—might have had something to do with the two deaths? Why? Had the parents forgotten to pay the fees?"

Blunt didn't smile. "Roscoe telephones me because he's worried about his son. The next day the man's dead. We've also learned from Russian intelligence sources that a week before he died, Ivanov had a violent argument with *his* son. Apparently Ivanov was worried about something. Now do you see the link?"

Alex thought for a moment. "So you want me to go and look into this school," he said. "How are you going to manage that? I don't have parents, and they were never rich anyway."

"We've already arranged for that," Mrs. Jones said, and Alex realized that she must have made her plans before the business with the crane ever happened. Even if he hadn't drawn attention to himself, they would have come for him. "We're going to supply you with a wealthy father. His name is Sir David Friend."

"Friend . . . as in Friends Supermarkets?" Alex had seen the name often enough in the newspapers.

"Supermarkets. Department stores. Art galleries. Soccer teams." Mrs. Jones paused. "Friend is certainly a member of the same club as Roscoe. The billionaires' club. He's also heavily involved in government circles, as personal adviser to the prime minister. Very little happens in this country without Sir David being involved in some way."

"We've created a false identity for you," Blunt said. "From this moment on, I want you to start thinking of yourself as Alex Friend, the fourteen-year-old son of Sir David. You've been expelled from Eton. You have a criminal record . . . shoplifting, vandalism, and possession of drugs. Sir David and his wife, Caroline, don't know what to do with you. So they've enrolled you in the academy. And you've been accepted."

"Isn't school vacation about to start?"

"They don't have official vacations. The school is open all year round."

"And Sir David has agreed to all this?" Alex asked.

Blunt sniffed. "As a matter of fact, he wasn't very happy about it—about using someone as young as you. But I spoke to him at some length and yes, he agreed to help."

"So when am I going to the academy?"

"Five days from now," Mrs. Jones said. "But first you have to immerse yourself in your new life. When you leave here, we've arranged for you to be taken to Sir David's home. He has a house in Lancashire. He lives there with his wife, and he has a daughter. She's one year older than you. You'll spend the rest of the week with the family, which should give you time to learn everything you need to know. It's vital that you have a strong cover. After that, you'll leave for Grenoble."

"And what do I do when I get there?"

"We'll give you a full briefing nearer the time. Essentially, your job is to find out everything you can. It may be that this school is perfectly ordinary and that there was in fact no connection between the deaths. If so, we'll pull you out. But we want to be sure."

"How will I get in touch with you?"

"We'll arrange all that." Mrs. Jones ran an eye over Alex, then turned to Blunt. "We'll have to do something about his appearance," she said. "He doesn't exactly look the part."

"See to it!" Blunt said.

Alex sighed. It was strange, really. He was simply going from one school to another, from a London comprehensive to a finishing school in France. It wasn't quite the adventure he'd been hoping for.

He stood up and followed Mrs. Jones out of the room. As he left, Blunt was already sifting through his documents as if he'd forgotten that Alex had been there or even existed.

5

THE SHOOTING PARTY

THE CHAUFFEUR-DRIVEN Rolls-Royce Corniche cruised along a tree-lined avenue, penetrating ever deeper into the Lancashire countryside, its 6.75-liter light pressure V8 engine barely a whisper in the great, green silence all around. Alex sat in the back, trying to be unimpressed by this car that cost as much as a house. Forget the plush carpeting, the wooden panels, and the leather seats, he told himself. It's only a car.

It was the day after his meeting at MI6, and, as Alan Blunt had ordered, his appearance had completely changed. He had to look like a rebel, the rich son who wanted to live life by his own rules. So Alex had been dressed in purposefully provocative clothes. He was wearing a T-shirt cut so low that most of his chest was exposed, and there was a leather thong around his neck. A baggy, checked shirt, missing most of its buttons, hung off his shoulders and down to his faded Tommy Hilfiger jeans, frayed at the knees and ankles. Despite his protests, his hair had been cut so short that he almost looked like a skinhead, and his right ear had been pierced. He could still feel it throbbing underneath the temporary stud that had been put in to keep the hole from closing.

The car had reached a set of wrought iron gates, which opened automatically to receive it. And there was Haverstock Hall, a great mansion with stone figures on the terrace and seven figures in the price. Sir David's family had lived here for generations, Mrs. Jones had told him. They also seemed to own half the Lancashire countryside. The grounds stretched for miles in every direction, with sheep dotted across the hills on one side and three horses watching from an enclosure on the other. The house itself was Georgian: white brick with slender windows and columns. Everything looked very neat. There was a walled garden with evenly spaced beds, a square glass conservatory housing a swimming pool, and a series of ornamental hedges with every leaf perfectly in place.

The car stopped. The horses swung their necks around to watch Alex get out, their tails rhythmically beating at flies. Nothing else moved.

The chauffeur walked around to the trunk. "Sir

David will be inside," he said. He had disapproved of
Alex from the moment he set eyes on him. Of course,
he hadn't said as much. But he was a professional.
He could show it with his eyes.

Alex moved away from the car, drawn toward the
conservatory on the other side of the drive. It was a
warm day, the sun beating down on the glass, and the
water on the other side looked suddenly inviting. He
passed through an open set of doors. It was hot inside
the conservatory. The smell of chlorine rose up from
the water, stifling him.

He had thought that the pool was empty, but as he
watched, a figure swam up from the bottom, breaking
through the surface just in front of him. It was a girl,
dressed only in a white bikini. She had long, black hair
and dark eyes, but her skin was pale. Alex guessed she
must be fifteen years old and remembered what Mrs.
Jones had told him about Sir David Friend. "He has
a daughter . . . a year older than you." So this must
be her. He watched her heave herself out of the water. Her body was well shaped, closer to the woman
she would become than the girl she had been. She was
going to be beautiful. That much was certain. The
trouble was, she already knew it. When she looked at
Alex, arrogance flashed in her eyes.

"Who are you?" she asked. "What are you doing in here?"

"I'm Alex."

"Oh, yes." She reached for a towel and wrapped it around her neck. "Daddy said you were coming, but I didn't expect you just to walk in like this." Her voice was very adult and upper class. It sounded strange, coming out of that fifteen-year-old mouth. "Do you swim?" she asked.

"Yes," Alex said.

"That's a shame. I don't like having to share the pool. Especially with a boy. And a smelly London boy at that." She ran her eyes over Alex, taking in the torn jeans, the shaven hair, the stud in his ear. She shuddered. "I can't think what Daddy was doing, agreeing to let you stay," she went on. "And having to pretend you're my brother! What a ghastly idea! If I did have a brother, I can assure you he wouldn't look like *you*."

Alex was wondering whether to pick the girl up and throw her back into the pool or out through a window when there was a movement behind him, and he turned to see a tall, rather aristocratic man with curling gray hair and glasses, wearing a sports jacket, open-neck shirt, and cords, standing just behind him. He too seemed a little jolted by Alex's appearance, but he recovered quickly, extending a hand. "Alex?" he demanded.

"Yes."

"I'm David Friend."

Alex shook his hand. "How do you do," he said politely.

"I hope you had a good journey. I see you've met my daughter." He smiled at the girl, who was now sitting beside the pool, drying herself and ignoring them both.

"We haven't actually introduced ourselves," Alex said.

"Her name is Fiona."

"Fiona Friend." Alex smiled. "That's not a name I'll forget."

"I'm sure the two of you will get along fine." Sir David didn't sound convinced. He gestured back toward the house. "Why don't we go and talk in the study?"

Alex followed him back across the drive and into the house. The front door opened into a hall that could have come straight out of the pages of an expensive magazine. Everything was perfect, the antique furniture, ornaments, and paintings placed exactly so. There wasn't a speck of dust to be seen and even the sunlight, streaming in through the windows, seemed almost artificial, as if it was there only to bring out the best in everything it touched. It was the house of a man who knows exactly what he wants and has the time and money to get it.

"Nice place," Alex said.

"Thank you. Please come this way." Sir David opened a heavy, oak-paneled door to reveal a sophisticated and modern office beyond. There was a desk and two chairs, a pair of computers, a white leather sofa, and a series of metal bookshelves. Sir David motioned at the chair and sat down behind the desk.

He was unsure of himself. Alex could see it immediately. Sir David Friend might run a business empire worth millions—even billions—of dollars, but this was a new experience for him. Having Alex here, knowing who and what he was, he wasn't quite sure how to react.

"I've been told very little about you," he began. "Alan Blunt got in touch with me and asked me to put you up here for the rest of the week, to pretend that you're my son. I have to say, you don't look anything like me."

"I don't look anything like myself either," Alex said.

"You're on your way to some school in the French

Alps. They want you to investigate it." He paused. "Nobody asked me my opinion," he said, "but I'll give it to you anyway. I don't like the idea of a fourteen-year-old boy being used as a spy. It's dangerous—"

"I can look after myself," Alex cut in.

"I mean, it's dangerous to the government. If you manage to get yourself killed and anyone finds out, it could cause the prime minister a great deal of embarrassment." Sir David sighed. "I advised him against it, but for once he overruled me. It seems that the decision has already been made. This school—the academy—has already telephoned me to say that the assistant director will be coming here to pick you up next Saturday. It's a woman. A Mrs. Stellenbosch. That's a South African name, I think."

Sir David had a number of bulky files on his desk. He slid them forward. "In the meantime, I understand you have to familiarize yourself with details about my family. I've prepared a number of files. You'll also find information here about the school you're meant to have been expelled from—Eton. You can start reading them tonight." Alex took them and he went on. "If you need to know anything more, just ask. Fiona will be with you the whole time." He glanced down at his fingertips. "I'm sure that in itself will be quite an experience for you."

The door opened and a woman came in. She was slim with dark hair, very much like her daughter. She was wearing a simple mauve dress with a string of pearls around her neck. "David," she began, then stopped, seeing Alex.

"This is my wife," Friend said. "Caroline, this is the boy I was telling you about. Alex."

"It's very nice to meet you, Alex." Lady Caroline tried to smile but her lips managed only a faint twitch. "I understand you're going to stay with us for a while."

"Yes, Mother," Alex said.

Lady Caroline blushed.

"He has to pretend to be our son," Sir David reminded her. He turned to Alex. "Fiona doesn't know anything about MI6 and the rest of it. I don't want to alarm her. I've told her that it's connected with my work . . . a social experiment, if you like. She's to pretend you're her brother, to give you a week in the country as part of the family. I'd prefer it if you didn't tell her the truth."

"Dinner is in half an hour," Lady Caroline said.

"Do you eat venison?" She sniffed. "Perhaps you'd like to shower before you eat? I'll show you to your room."

Sir David stood up. "You've got a lot of reading to do. I'm afraid I have to go back to London tomorrow—I have lunch with the president of France—so I won't be able to help you. But, as I say, if there's anything you don't know . . ."

"Fiona Friend," Alex said.

Alex had been given a small, comfortable room at the back of the house. He took a quick shower, then put his old clothes back on again. He liked to feel clean but he had to look grimy—it suited the character of the boy he was supposed to be. He opened the first of the files. Sir David had been thorough. He had given Alex the names and recent histories of just about the entire family, as well as photographs of vacations, details of the house and stables in Mayfair, the apartments in New York, Paris, and Rome, and the villa in Barbados. There were newspaper clippings, magazine articles . . . everything he could possibly need.

A gong sounded. It was seven o'clock. Alex went downstairs and into the dining room. The room had six windows and a polished mahogany table long enough to seat fifteen. But only the three of them were there: Sir David, Lady Caroline, and Fiona. The food had already been served, presumably by a butler or cook. Sir David gestured at an empty chair. Alex sat down.

"Fiona was just talking about Soloman," Lady Caroline said. There was a pause. "Soloman is a horse. We have lots of horses." She turned to Alex. "Do you ride?"

"Only my bicycle," Alex said.

"I'm sure Alex isn't interested in horses," Fiona said. She appeared to be in a bad mood. "In fact, I doubt if we have anything in common. Why do I have to pretend he's my brother? The whole thing is completely—"

"Fiona . . . ," Sir David muttered in a low voice.

"Well, it's all very well having him here, Daddy, but it *is* meant to be *my* Easter vacation." Alex realized that Fiona must go to a private school. Her term would have ended earlier than his. "I don't think it's fair."

"Alex is here because of my work," Sir David continued. It was strange, Alex thought, the way they talked about him as if he weren't actually there. "I know you have a lot of questions, Fiona, but you're

just going to have to do as I say. He's with us only until the end of the week. I want you to look after him."

"But he's a city boy!" Fiona insisted. "He's going
to hate it here. And anyway, how can pretending he's
my brother help you with your supermarkets?"

"Fiona . . ." Sir David didn't want any more argument. "It's what I told you. An experiment. And
you will make him feel welcome!"

Fiona picked up her glass and looked directly at
Alex for the first time since he had come into the
room. "We'll see about that," she said.

The week seemed endless. After only two days, Alex
was beginning to think that Fiona was right. He was
a city boy. He had lived his whole life in London and
felt utterly lost, suffocating in the big green blanket of
the countryside. The estate went on for as far as the
eye could see, and the Friends seemed to have no connection with the real world. Alex had never felt more
isolated. Sir David himself had disappeared to London. Lady Caroline did her best to avoid Alex. Once
or twice she drove into Skipton—the nearest town—
but otherwise she seemed to spend a lot of time gar-
dening or arranging flowers. And Fiona . . .

She had made it clear from the start how much she disliked Alex. There could be no reason for this. It was simply that he was an outsider, and Fiona seemed to mistrust anything that didn't belong to the miniature world of Haverstock Hall. She'd asked him several times what he was really doing there. Alex had shrugged and said nothing, which had only made her dislike him all the more.

And then, on the third day, she introduced him to some of her friends.

"I'm going shooting," she told him. "I don't suppose you want to come?"

Alex shrugged. He had memorized most of the details in the files and figured he could easily pass as a member of the family. Now he was counting the hours until the woman from the academy arrived to take him away.

"Have you ever been shooting?" Fiona asked.

"No," Alex said.

"I go hunting and shooting," Fiona said. "But of course, you're a city boy. You wouldn't understand."

"What's so great about killing animals?" Alex asked.

"It's part of the country way of life. It's tradition."

Fiona looked at him as if he were stupid. It was how she always looked at him. "Anyway, the animals enjoy it."

The shooting party turned out to be young and—apart from Fiona—entirely male. Five of them were waiting on the edge of a forest that was part of the Haverstock estate. Rufus, the leader, was sixteen and well built with dark, curling hair. He seemed to be Fiona's boyfriend. The others—Henry, Max, Bartholomew, and Fred—were about the same age. Alex looked at them with a heavy heart. They had uniform Barbour jackets, tweed trousers, flat caps, and Huntsman leather boots. They spoke with uniform upper-class accents. Each of them carried a shotgun, with the barrel broken over his arm. Two of them were smoking. They gazed at Alex with barely concealed contempt. Fiona must have already told them about him. The city boy.

Quickly, she made the introductions. Rufus stepped forward.

"Nice to have you with us," he drawled. He ran his eyes over Alex, not bothering to hide his contempt. "Up for a bit of shooting, are you?"

"I don't have a gun," Alex said.

"Well, I'm afraid I'm not going to lend you mine."

Rufus snapped the barrel back into place and held it up for Alex to see. It was a beautiful gun, with twenty-five inches of gleaming steel stretching out of a dark walnut stock decorated with ornately carved, solid silver sideplates. "It's an over-and-under shotgun with detachable trigger lock, handmade by Abbiatico and Salvinelli," he said. "It cost me thirty grand—or my mother, anyway. It was a birthday present."

"It couldn't have been easy to wrap," Alex said. "Where did she put the ribbon?"

Rufus's smile faded. "You wouldn't know anything about guns," he said. He nodded at one of the other teenagers, who handed Alex a much more ordinary weapon. It was old and a little rusty. "You can use this one," he said. "And if you're very good and don't get in the way, maybe we'll let you have a bullet."

They all laughed at that. Then the two smokers put out their cigarettes and everyone set off into the woods.

Thirty minutes later, Alex knew he had made a mistake in coming. The boys blasted away left and right, aiming at anything that moved. A rabbit spun in a glistening red ball. A wood pigeon tumbled out of the branches and flapped around on the leaves below. Whatever the quality of their weapons, the teenagers weren't good shots. The animals they managed to hit were only wounded, and Alex felt a growing sickness, following this trail of blood.

They reached a clearing and paused to reload. Alex turned to Fiona. "I'm going back to the house," he said.

"Why? Can't stand the sight of a little blood?"

Alex glanced at a hare about fifty feet away. It was lying on its side with its back legs kicking helplessly. "I'm surprised they let you carry guns," he said. "I thought you had to be seventeen."

Rufus overheard him. He stepped forward, an ugly look in his eyes. "We don't bother with rules in the countryside," he muttered.

"Maybe Alex wants to call a policeman!" Fiona said.

"The nearest police station is forty miles from here," Rufus said with a cold smile.

"Do you want to borrow my cell phone?" one of the other boys asked.

They all laughed again. Alex had had enough. Without saying another word, he turned around and walked off.

It had taken him thirty minutes to reach the clearing, but thirty minutes later he was still stuck in the woods, completely surrounded by trees and wild shrubs. Alex realized he was lost. He was annoyed with himself. He should have watched where he was going when he was following Fiona and the others. The forest was enormous. Walk in the wrong direction and he might blunder onto the North Yorkshire moors . . . and it could be days before he was found. At the same time, the spring foliage was so thick that he could barely see ten yards in any direction. How could he possibly find his way? Should he try to retrace his steps or continue forward in the hope of stumbling on the right path?

Alex sensed danger before the first shot was fired. Perhaps it was the snapping of a twig or the click of a metal bolt being slipped into place. He froze—and that was what saved him. There was an explosion— loud, close—and a tree one step ahead of him shattered, splinters of wood dancing in the air.

Alex turned around, searching for whoever had fired the shot. "What are you doing?" he shouted. "You nearly hit me!"

Almost immediately there was a second shot and, just behind it, a whoop of excited laughter. And then

Alex realized what was happening: They hadn't mistaken him for an animal. They were aiming at him for fun.

He dived forward and began to run. The trunks of the trees seemed to press in on him from all sides, threatening to bar his way. The ground underneath was soft from recent rain and dragged at his feet, trying to glue them into place. There was a third explosion. He ducked, feeling the gunshot spray above his head, shredding the foliage.

Anywhere else in the world, this would have been madness. But this was the middle of the English countryside and these were rich, bored teenagers who were used to having things their own way. Somehow, Alex had insulted them. Perhaps it had been the jibe about the wrapping paper. Perhaps it was his refusal to tell Fiona who he really was. But they had decided to teach him a lesson, and they would worry about the consequences later. Did they mean to kill him? "We don't bother with rules in the countryside," Rufus had said. If Alex was badly wounded—or even killed—they would somehow get away with it. *A dreadful accident. He wasn't looking where he was going and stepped into the line of fire.*

No. That was impossible.

They were trying to scare him—that was all.

Two more shots. A pheasant erupted out of the ground, a ball of spinning feathers, and screamed up into the sky. Alex ran on, his breath rasping in his throat. A thick briar reached out across his chest and tore at his clothes. He still had the gun he had been given, and he used it to beat a way through. A tangle of roots almost sent him sprawling.

"Alex? Where are you?" The voice belonged to Rufus. It was high-pitched and mocking, coming from the other side of a barrier of leaves. There was another shot, but this one went high over his head. They couldn't see him. Had he escaped?

No, he hadn't. Alex came to a stumbling, sweating halt. He had broken out of the woods but he was still hopelessly lost. Worse—he was trapped. He had come to the edge of a wide, filthy lake. The water was a scummy brown and looked almost solid. No ducks or wild birds came anywhere near the surface. The evening sun beat down on it and the smell of decay drifted up.

"He went that way!"

"No . . . through here!"

"Let's try the lake."

Alex heard the voices and knew that he couldn't let

them find him here. He had a sudden image of his body, weighed down with stones, at the bottom of the lake. But that gave him an idea. He had to hide.

He stepped into the water. He would need something to breathe through. He had seen people do this in films. They would lie in the water and breathe through a hollow reed. But there were no reeds here. Apart from grass and thick, slimy algae, nothing was growing at all.

One minute later, Rufus appeared at the edge of the lake, his gun still hooked over his arm. He stopped and looked around with eyes that knew the forest well. Nothing moved.

"He must have doubled back," he said.

The other hunters had gathered behind him. There was tension between them now, a guilty silence. They knew the game had gone too far.

"Let's forget him," one of them said.

"Yeah . . ."

"We've taught him a lesson."

They were in a hurry to get home. As one, they disappeared back the way they had come. Rufus was left on his own, still clutching his gun, searching for Alex. He took one last look across the water, then turned to follow them.

That was when Alex struck. He had been lying under the water, watching the vague shapes of the teenagers as if through a sheet of thick brown glass. The barrel of the shotgun was in his mouth. The rest of the gun was just above the surface of the lake. He was using the hollow tubes to breathe. Now he rose up—a nightmare creature oozing mud and water, with fury in his eyes. Rufus heard him but he was too late. Alex swung the shotgun, catching Rufus in the small of the back. Rufus grunted and fell to his knees, his own gun falling out of his hands. Alex picked it up. There were two cartridges in the breech. He snapped the gun shut.

Rufus looked at him, and suddenly all the arrogance had gone and he was just a stupid, frightened teenager, struggling to get to his knees.

"Alex . . ." The single word came out as a whimper. It was as if he were seeing Alex for the first time. "I'm sorry!" he sniveled. "We weren't really going to hurt you. It was a joke. Fiona put us up to it. We just wanted to scare you. Please . . ."

Alex paused, breathing heavily. "How do I get out of here?" he asked.

"Just follow the lake around," Rufus said. "There's a path."

Rufus was still on his knees. There were tears in his eyes. Alex realized that he was pointing the silver-plated shotgun in his direction. He turned it away, disgusted with himself. This boy wasn't the enemy. He was nothing.

"Don't follow me," Alex said and began to walk.

"Please!" Rufus called after him. "Can I have my gun back? My mother would kill me if I lost it."

Alex stopped. He weighed the weapon in his hands, then threw it with all his strength. The hand-crafted Italian shotgun spun twice in the dying light, then disappeared with a splash in the middle of the lake. "You're too young to play with guns," he said.

He walked away, letting the forest swallow him up.

6

THE TUNNEL

THE MAN SITTING IN THE gold, antique chair turned his head slowly and gazed out the window at the snow-covered slopes of Point Blanc. Dr. Hugo Grief was almost sixty years old with short, white hair and a face that was almost colorless too. His skin was white, his lips vague shadows. Even his tongue was no more than gray. And yet, against this blank background, he wore circular wire glasses with dark red lenses. For him, the entire world would be the color of blood. He had long fingers, the nails beautifully manicured. He was dressed in a dark suit buttoned up to his neck. If there were such a thing as a vampire, it might look very much like Dr. Hugo Grief.

"I have decided to move the Gemini Project into its last phase," he said. He spoke with a South African accent, biting into each word before it left his mouth. "There can be no further delay."

"I understand, Dr. Grief."

A woman sat opposite Dr. Grief, dressed in tight-fitting spandex with a sweatband around her head. This was Eva Stellenbosch. She had just finished her morning workout—two hours of weight lifting and aerobics—and was still breathing heavily, her huge muscles rising and falling. Mrs. Stellenbosch had a facial structure that wasn't quite human, with lips curving out far in front of her nose and wisps of bright ginger hair hanging over a high-domed forehead. She was holding a glass filled with some milky green liquid. Her fingers were thick and stubby. She had to be careful not to break the glass.

She sipped her drink, then frowned. "Are you sure we're ready?" she asked.

"We have no choice in the matter. We have had two unsatisfactory results in the last few months. First Ivanov. Then Roscoe in New York. Quite apart from the expense of arranging the terminations, it's possible that someone may have connected the two deaths."

"Possible, but unlikely," Mrs. Stellenbosch said.

"The intelligence services are idle and inefficient, it is true. The CIA in America. MI6 in England. Even the KGB. They're all shadows of what they used to be. But even so, there's always the chance that one of them might have accidentally stumbled onto something. The sooner we end this phase of the operation, the more chance we have of remaining unnoticed." Dr. Grief brought his hands together and rested his chin on his fingers. "When is the final boy arriving?" he asked.

"Alex?" Mrs. Stellenbosch sipped from her cup and set it down. She opened her handbag and took out a handkerchief, which she used to wipe her lips. "I am traveling to England tomorrow," she said.

"Excellent. You'll take the boy to Paris on the way here?"

"Of course, Doctor. If that's what you wish."

"It is very much what I wish. We can do all the preliminary work there. It will save time. What about the Sprintz boy?"

"I'm afraid we still need another few days."

"That means that he and Alex will be here at the same time."

"Yes."

Dr. Grief considered. He had to balance the risk of the two boys meeting against the dangers of moving too fast. It was fortunate that he had a scientific mind. His calculations were never wrong. "Very well," he said. "The Sprintz boy can stay with us for another few days. I sense he is growing restless, and a new friend might put his mind at ease."

Mrs. Stellenbosch nodded. She lifted her glass and emptied its contents, the veins in her neck throbbing as she swallowed.

"Alex Friend is an excellent catch for us," Dr. Grief said.

"Supermarkets?" The woman sounded unconvinced.

"His father has the prime minister's ear. He is an impressive man. His son, I am sure, will meet up to all our expectations." Dr. Grief smiled. His eyes glowed red. "Very soon, we'll have Alex here, at the academy. And then, at last, the Gemini Project will be complete."

"You're sitting all wrong," Fiona said. "Your back isn't straight. Your hands should be lower. And your feet are pointing the wrong way."

"What does it matter, so long as you're enjoying yourself?" Alex asked, speaking through gritted teeth.

It was the fourth day of his stay at Haverstock Hall, and Fiona had been persuaded to take him out riding. Alex wasn't enjoying himself at all. First he'd had to endure the inevitable lecture—although he had barely listened. The horses were Iberian or Hungarian. They'd won a bucketful of gold medals. Alex didn't care. All he knew was that his horse was big and black and attracted flies. And that he was riding it with all the style of a sack of potatoes on a trampoline.

The two of them had barely mentioned the business in the forest. When Alex had limped back to the house, soaked and freezing, Fiona had politely fetched him a towel and offered him a cup of tea.

"You tried to kill me!" Alex said.

"Don't be silly." Fiona looked at Alex with something like pity in her eyes. "We would never do that. Rufus is a very nice boy."

"What?"

"It was just a game, Alex. Just a bit of fun."

And that was it. Fiona had smiled as if everything had been explained and then gone to have a swim. Alex had spent the rest of the evening with the files. He was trying to take in a fake history that spanned fourteen years. There were uncles and aunts, friends at Eton, a whole crowd of people he had to know without ever having met any of them. More than that, he was trying to get the feel of this luxurious lifestyle.

That was why he was here now, out riding with Fiona—she upright in her riding jacket and breeches, he bumping along behind.

They had ridden for about an hour and a half when they came to a tunnel. Fiona had tried to teach Alex a bit of technique—the difference, for example, between walking, trotting, and cantering. But this was one sport he had already decided he would never take up. Every bone in his body had been rattled out of shape, and his bottom was so bruised he wondered if he would ever be able to sit down again. Fiona seemed to be enjoying his torment. He even wondered if she had chosen a particularly bumpy route to add to his bruises. Or maybe it was just a particularly bumpy horse.

There was a single railway line ahead of them, crossed by a tiny lane with an automatic gate crossing equipped with a bell and flashing lights to warn motorists of any approaching train. Fiona steered her horse—a smaller gray—toward it. Alex's horse automatically followed. He assumed they were going to cross the line, but when she reached the barrier, Fiona stopped.

"There's a shortcut we can take if you want to get home," she said.

"A shortcut would be good," Alex admitted.

"It's that way."

Fiona pointed up the line toward a tunnel, a gaping black hole in the side of a hill, surrounded by dark red brick. Alex looked at her to see if she was joking. She was obviously quite serious. He turned back to the tunnel. It was like the barrel of a gun, pointing at him, warning him to keep away. He could almost imagine the giant finger on the trigger, somewhere behind the hill. How long was it? Looking more carefully, he could see a pinprick of light at the other end, perhaps half a mile away.

"You're not serious," he said.

"Actually, Alex, I don't usually tell jokes. When I say something, I mean it. I'm just like my father."

"Except your father isn't completely crazy," Alex muttered.

Fiona pretended not to hear him. "The tunnel is about one mile long," she explained. "There's a bridge on the other side, then another gate crossing. If we go that way, we can be home in thirty minutes. Otherwise it's an hour and a half back the way we came."

"Then let's go the way we came."

"Oh, Alex, don't be such a scaredy-cat!" Fiona pouted at him. "There's only one train an hour on this line and the next one isn't due for . . ." She looked at her watch. ". . . twenty minutes. I've been through the tunnel a hundred times and it never takes more than five minutes. Less if you canter."

"It's still crazy to ride on a railway line."

"Well, you'll have to find your own way home if you turn back." She kicked with her heels and her horse jerked forward, past the barrier and onto the line. "I'll see you later."

But Alex followed her. He would never have been able to ride back to the house on his own. He didn't know the way, and he could barely control his horse. Even now it was following Fiona with no prompting from him. Would the two animals really enter the darkness of the tunnel? It seemed incredible, but Fiona had said they had done it before, and sure enough, the horses walked into the side of the hill without even hesitating.

Alex shivered as the light was suddenly cut off behind him. It was cold and clammy inside. The air smelled of soot and diesel. The tunnel was a natural echo chamber. The horses' hooves rattled all around them as they struck against the gravel between the ties. What if his horse stumbled? Alex put the thought out of his mind. The leather saddles creaked. Slowly his eyes got used to the dark. A certain amount of sunshine was filtering in from behind. More comfortingly, the way out was clearly visible straight ahead, the circle of light widening with every step. He tried to relax. Perhaps this wasn't going to be so bad after all.

And then Fiona spoke. She had slowed down, allowing his horse to catch up with hers. "Are you still worried about the train, Alex?" she said scornfully. "Perhaps you'd like to go faster."

He heard the riding crop whistle through the air and felt his horse jerk as Fiona whipped it hard on the rear. The horse whinnied and leapt forward. Alex was almost thrown backward off the saddle. Digging in with his legs, he just managed to cling on, but the whole top of his body was at a crazy angle, the reins tearing into the horse's mouth. Fiona laughed. And then Alex was aware only of the wind rushing past him, the thick blackness spinning around his face, and the horses' hooves striking heavily at the gravel as the animal careened forward. Soot blew into his eyes, blinding him. He thought he was going to fall. Minutes seemed to pass in mere seconds.

But then, miraculously, they burst out into the light. Alex fought for his balance and then brought the horse back under control, pulling back with the reins and squeezing the horse's flanks with his knees. He took a deep breath and waited for Fiona to appear.

His horse had come to rest on the bridge that she had mentioned. The bridge was fashioned out of thick iron girders and spanned a river. There had been a lot of rain that month and, about fifty feet below him, the water was racing past, dark green and deep. Carefully, he turned around to face the tunnel. If he lost control here, it would be easy to fall over the edge. The sides of the bridge couldn't have been more than three feet high.

He could hear Fiona approaching. She had been cantering after him, probably laughing the entire way. He gazed into the tunnel, and that was when Fiona's gray horse burst out, raced past him, and disappeared through the gate crossing on the other side of the bridge.

But Fiona wasn't on it.

The horse had come out alone.

It took Alex a few seconds to work it out. His head was reeling. She must have fallen off. Perhaps her horse had stumbled. She could be lying inside the tunnel. On the track. How long was there until the next train? Twenty minutes, she had said. But at least five of those minutes had gone, and she might have been exaggerating to begin with.

Alex swore. Damn this wretched girl with her spoiled brat behavior and her almost suicidal games. But he couldn't leave her. He seized hold of the reins. Somehow he would get this horse to obey him. He had to get her out, and he had to do it fast.

Perhaps his desperation managed to communicate itself to the horse's brain. The animal wheeled around and tried to back away, but when Alex kicked with his heels, it stumbled forward and reluctantly entered the darkness of the tunnel for a second time. Alex kicked again. He didn't want to hurt it, but he could think of no other way to make it obey him.

The horse trotted on. Alex searched ahead. "Fiona!" he called out. There was no reply. He had hoped that she would be walking toward him, but he couldn't hear any footsteps. If only there were more light!

The horse stopped and there she was, right in front of him, lying on the ground, her arms and chest actually on the line. If a train came now, it would cut her in half. It was too dark to see her face, but when she spoke he heard the pain in her voice.

"Alex . . . ," she said. "I think I've broken my ankle."

"What happened?"

"There was a cobweb or something. I was trying to keep up with you. It went in my face and I lost my balance."

She'd been trying to keep up with him! She almost sounded as if she were blaming him—as if she had forgotten that she was the one who had whipped his horse on in the first place.

"Can you get up?" Alex asked.

"I don't think so."

Alex sighed. Keeping a tight hold on the reins, he slid off his horse. Fiona had fallen right in the middle of the tunnel. He forced himself not to panic. If what she had told him was true, the next train must still be at least ten minutes away. He reached down to help her up. His foot came to rest on one of the rails . . .

. . . and he felt something. Under his foot. Shivering up his leg. The track was vibrating.

The train was on its way.

"You've got to stand up," he said, trying to keep the fear out of his voice. He could already see the train in his imagination, thundering along the line. When it plunged into the tunnel, it would be a five-hundred-ton torpedo that would smash them to pieces. He could hear the grinding of the wheels, the roar of the engines. Blood and darkness. It would be a horrible way to die.

But he still had time.

"Can you move your toes?" he asked.

"I think so." Fiona was clutching him.

"Then your ankle's probably sprained, not broken. Come on."

He dragged her up, wondering if it would be possible to stay inside the tunnel, on the edge of the track. If they hugged the wall, the train might simply go past them. But Alex knew there wouldn't be enough space. And even if the train missed them, it would still hit the horse. Suppose it derailed? Dozens of people could be killed.

"What train comes this way?" he asked. "Does it carry passengers?"

"Yes." Fiona was sounding tearful. "It's a Virgin train. Heading up to Glasgow."

Alex sighed. It was just his luck to get the only Virgin train ever to arrive on time.

Fiona froze. "What's that?" she asked.

She had heard the clanging of a bell. The gate crossing! It was signaling the approach of the train, the barrier lowering itself over the road.

And then Alex heard a second sound that made his blood run cold. For a moment he couldn't breathe. It was extraordinary. His breath was stuck in his lungs and refused to get up to his mouth. His whole body was paralyzed as if some switch had been thrown in his brain. He was simply terrified.

The screech of a train whistle. It was still a mile or more away, but the tunnel was acting as a sound conductor and he could feel it cutting into him. And then another sound: the rolling thunder of the diesel engine. It was moving fast toward them. Underneath his foot, the rail vibrated more violently.

Alex gulped for air and forced his legs to obey him. "Get on the horse," he shouted. "I'll help you."

Not caring how much pain he caused her, he dragged Fiona next to the horse and forced her up onto the saddle. The noise grew louder with every second that passed. The rail was humming softly, like a giant tuning fork. The very air inside the tunnel seemed to be in motion, spinning left and right as if trying to get out of the way.

Fiona squealed and Alex felt her weight leave his

arms as she fell onto the saddle. The horse whinnied and took a half step sideways, and for a dreadful moment Alex thought she was going to ride off without him. There was just enough light to make out the shapes of both the animal and its rider. He saw Fiona grabbing the reins. She brought it back under control. Alex reached up and caught hold of the horse's mane. He used the thick hair to pull himself onto the saddle, in front of Fiona. The noise of the train was getting louder and louder. Soot and loose concrete were trickling out of the curving walls. The wind currents were twisting faster, the rails singing. For a moment the two of them were tangled together, but then he had the reins and she was clinging on to him, her arms around his chest.

"Go!" he shouted and kicked the horse.

The horse needed no encouragement. It raced for the light, galloping up the railway line, throwing Alex and Fiona back and forward, into each other.

Alex didn't dare look behind him, but he felt the train as it reached the mouth of the tunnel and plunged in, traveling at 105 miles per hour. A shock wave hammered into them. The train was punching the air out of its way, filling the space with solid steel. The horse understood the danger and burst forward with new speed, its hooves flying over the ties in great strides. Ahead of them the tunnel mouth opened up, but Alex knew, with a sickening sense of despair, that they weren't going to make it. Even when they got out of the tunnel, they would still be hemmed in by the sides of the bridge. The second gate crossing was a hundred yards farther down the line. They might get out but they would die in the open air.

The horse passed through the end of the tunnel. Alex felt the circle of darkness slip over his shoulders. Fiona was screaming, her arms wrapped around him so tightly that he could barely breathe. He could hardly hear her. The roar of the train was right behind him, and as the horse began a desperate race over the bridge, he sneaked a glance around. He just had time to see the huge, metallic beast roar out of the tunnel, towering over them, its body painted the brilliant red of the Virgin colors, the driver staring in horror from behind his window. There was a second blast from the train whistle, this one all-consuming, exploding all around them. Alex knew what he had to do. He pulled on one rein, at the same time kicking with the opposite foot. He just had to hope the horse would understand what he wanted.

And somehow it worked. The horse veered around. Now it was facing the side of the bridge. There was a final, deafening blast from the train. Diesel fumes smothered them. Alex kicked again with all his strength. The horse jumped.

The train roared past, missing them by inches. But now they were in the air, over the side of the bridge. The railcars were still thundering past, a red blur. Fiona screamed a second time. Everything seemed to be happening in slow motion as they fell. One moment they were next to the bridge, a moment later underneath it and still falling. The green river rose up to receive them.

The horse with its two riders plummeted through the air and crashed into the river. Alex just had time to snatch a breath. He was afraid that the water wouldn't be deep enough, that all three of them would end up with broken necks. But they hit the surface and passed through, down into a freezing, dark green whirlpool that sucked at them greedily, threatening to keep them there forever. Fiona was torn away from him. He felt the horse kick itself free. Bubbles exploded out of his mouth and he realized he was yelling.

Finally, Alex rose to the surface again. The water was rushing past and, dragged back by his clothes and shoes, he clumsily swam for the nearest bank.

The train driver hadn't stopped. Perhaps he had been too frightened by what had happened. Perhaps he wanted to pretend it hadn't happened at all. Either way, the train had gone. Alex reached the bank and pulled himself, shivering, onto the grass. There was a splutter and a cough from behind him, and Fiona appeared. She had lost her riding hat, and her long black hair was hanging over her face. Alex looked past her. The horse had also managed to reach dry land. It trotted forward and shook itself, seemingly unharmed. Alex was glad about that. When all was said and done, the horse had saved both their lives.

He stood up. Water dripped out of his clothes. There was no feeling anywhere in his body. He wondered whether it was because of the cold water or the shock of what he had just been through. He went over to Fiona and helped her to her feet.

"Are you all right?" he asked.

"Yes." She was looking at him strangely. She wobbled, and he put out a hand to steady her. "Thank you," she said.

"That's all right."

"No." She held on to his hand. Her shirt had fallen open and she threw back her head, shaking the hair out of her eyes. "What you did back there . . . it was fantastic. Alex, I'm sorry I've been so awful to you all week. I thought—because you were here only for charity and all the rest of it—I thought you were just an oik. But I was wrong about you. You're really great. And I know we're going to be friends now." She half closed her eyes and moved toward him, her lips slightly parted. "You can kiss me if you like," she said.

Alex let go of her and turned away. "Thanks, Fiona," he said. "But frankly I'd prefer to kiss the horse."

7

SPECIAL EDITION

THE HELICOPTER CIRCLED twice over Haverstock Hall before beginning its descent. It was a Robinson R44, four-seater aircraft, American built. There was only one person—the pilot—inside. Sir David Friend had returned from London, and he and his wife came outside to watch it land in front of the house. The engine noise died down and the rotors began to slow. The cabin door slid open, and the pilot got out, dressed in a one-piece leather flying suit, helmet, and goggles.

The pilot walked up to them, extending a hand. "Good morning," she shouted over the noise of the rotors. "I'm Mrs. Stellenbosch. From the academy . . ."

If Sir David and Lady Caroline had been thrown by their first sight of Alex, the appearance of the assistant director left them frozen to the spot. Sir David was the first to recover. "You flew the helicopter yourself?"

"Yes . . . I'm qualified," Mrs. Stellenbosch answered.

"Would you like to come in?" Lady Caroline said. "Perhaps you'd like some tea."

She led them into the house and into the living room, where Mrs. Stellenbosch sat, legs apart, her helmet on the sofa beside her. Sir David and Lady Caroline sat opposite her. Tea had been brought in on a tray.

"Do you mind if I smoke?" Mrs. Stellenbosch asked. She reached into a pocket and took out a small packet of cigars without waiting for an answer. She lit one and blew smoke. "What a very beautiful house you have, Sir David. Georgian, I would say, but decorated with such taste! And where, may I ask, is Alex?"

"He went for a walk," Sir David said.

"Perhaps he's a little nervous." She smiled again and took the teacup Lady Caroline had proffered. "I understand that Alex has been a great source of concern to you."

Sir David Friend nodded. His eyes gave nothing away. For the next few minutes, he told Mrs. Stellenbosch about Alex, how he had been expelled from Eton, how out of control he had become. Lady

Caroline listened to all this in silence, occasionally holding her husband's arm.

"I'm at my wit's end," Sir David concluded. "We have an older daughter, and she's perfectly delightful. But Alex? He hangs around the house. He doesn't read. He doesn't show any interest in anything. His appearance . . . well, you'll see for yourself. The Point Blanc Academy is our last resort, Mrs. Stellenbosch. We're desperately hoping you can straighten him out."

The assistant director poked at the air with her cigar, leaving a gray trail. "I'm sure you've been a marvelous father, Sir David," she purred. "But these modern children! It's heartbreaking the way some of them behave. You've done the right thing, coming to us. As I'm sure you know, the academy has had a remarkable success rate over the years."

"What exactly do you do?" Lady Caroline asked.

"We have our methods." The woman's eyes twinkled. She tapped ash into her saucer. "But I can promise you, we'll straighten out all his problems. Don't you worry! When he comes home, he'll be a completely different boy."

Alex had reached the edge of a field about a half mile from the house. He had seen the helicopter land and knew that his time had come. But he wasn't ready yet to leave. Mrs. Jones had telephoned him the night before. Once again, MI6 wasn't going to send him empty-handed into what might be enemy territory.

He watched as a combine harvester rumbled slowly toward him, cutting a swathe through the grass. It jerked to a halt a short distance away, and the door of the cabin opened. A man got out—with difficulty. He was so fat that he had to squeeze himself out, first one buttock, then the next, and finally his stomach, shoulders, and head. The man was wearing a checked shirt and blue overalls—a farmer's outfit. But even if he'd had a straw hat and a blade of corn between his teeth, Alex could never have imagined him actually farming anything.

The man grinned at him. "Hello, old chap!" he said.

"Hello, Mr. Smithers," Alex replied.

Smithers worked for MI6. He had supplied the various devices Alex had used on his last mission. "Very nice to see you again!" he exclaimed. He winked. "What do you think of the cover? I was told to blend in with the countryside."

"The combine harvester's a great idea," Alex said. "Except, this is April. There isn't anything to harvest."

"I hadn't thought of that!" Smithers beamed. "The trouble is, I'm not really a field agent. Field agent!" He looked around him and laughed. "Anyway, I'm jolly glad to have the chance to work with you again, Alex—to think up a few bits and pieces for you. It's not often I get a teenager. Much more fun than the adults!"

He reached into the cabin and pulled out a suitcase. "Actually, it's been a bit tricky this time," he went on.

"Have you got another Nintendo Game Boy?" Alex asked.

"No. That's just it. The school doesn't allow Game Boys—or any computers at all, for that matter. They supply their own laptops. I could have hidden a dozen gadgets inside a laptop, but there you are! Now, let's see. . . ." He opened the case. "I'm told there's still a lot of snow up at Point Blanc, so you'll need this."

"A ski suit," Alex said. That was what Smithers was holding.

"Yes. But it's highly insulated and also bullet-proof." He pulled out a pair of green-tinted goggles. "These are ski goggles. But in case you have to go anywhere at night, they're actually infrared. There's a battery concealed in the frame. Just press the switch and you'll be able to see about twenty yards, even if there's no moon."

Smithers reached into the case a second time. "Now, what else would a boy of your age have with him? Fortunately, you're allowed to take a Sony Discman, provided all the CDs are classical." He handed Alex the machine.

"So while people are shooting at me in the middle of the night, I get to listen to music," Alex said.

"Absolutely. Only don't play the Beethoven!" Smithers held up the disc. "The Discman converts into an electric saw. The CD is diamond-edged. It'll cut through just about anything—useful if you need to get out in a hurry. There's also a panic button I've built in. If you're in real trouble and you need help, just press FAST FORWARD three times. It'll send out a signal that our satellite will pick up. And then we can fast forward you out!"

"Thank you, Mr. Smithers," Alex said, but he was disappointed and it showed.

Smithers understood. "I know what you want," he said. "But you know you can't have it. No guns! Mr. Blunt is adamant. He thinks you're too young."

"Not too young to get killed, though."

"I know. So I've given it a bit of thought and

rustled up a couple of . . . defensive measures, so to speak. This is just between you and me, you understand. I'm not sure Mr. Blunt would approve."

He held out a hand. A gold ear stud lay in two pieces in the middle of his palm: a diamond shape for the front and a catch to hold it at the back. The stud looked tiny surrounded by so much flesh. "They told me you'd had your ear pierced," he said. "So I made you this. Be very careful after you've put it in. Bringing the two pieces together will activate it."

"Activate what?" Alex looked doubtful.

"The ear stud is a small but very powerful explosive device. Like a miniature grenade. Separating the two pieces again will set it off. Count to ten and it'll blow a hole in just about anything . . . or anyone, I should add."

"Just so long as it doesn't blow off my ear," Alex muttered.

"No, no. It's perfectly safe so long as the pieces remain attached." Smithers smiled. "And finally, I'm very pleased with this. It's exactly what you'd expect to find in a young boy's luggage, and I designed it especially for you." He had produced a book.

Alex took it. It was a hardcover edition of the latest Harry Potter book. "Thanks," he said. "But I've already read it."

"This is a special edition. There's a gun built into the spine, and the chamber is loaded with a stun dart. Just point it and press the author's name. It'll knock out an adult in less than five seconds."

Alex smiled. Smithers climbed back into the combine harvester. For a moment he seemed to have wedged himself permanently into the door, but then with a grunt he managed to go the whole way. "Good luck, old chap," he said. "Come back in one piece! I really do enjoy having you around!"

It was time to go.

Alex's luggage was being loaded into the helicopter, and he was standing next to his new parents, clutching the Harry Potter book. Eva Stellenbosch was waiting for him underneath the rotors. He had been shocked by her appearance, and at first he had tried to hide it. But then he'd relaxed. He didn't have to be polite. Alex Rider might have good manners, but Alex Friend wouldn't give a damn what she thought. He glanced at her scornfully now and noticed that she was watching him carefully as he said good-bye.

Once again, Sir David Friend acted his part perfectly. "Good-bye, Alex," he said. "You will write to us and let us know you're okay?"

"If you want," Alex said.

Lady Caroline moved forward and kissed him. Alex backed away from her as if embarrassed. He had to admit that she looked genuinely sad.

"Come, Alex!" Mrs. Stellenbosch was in a hurry to get away. She had told him that the helicopter had a range of only four hundred miles and that they would need to stop in Paris to refuel.

And then Fiona appeared, crossing the grass toward them. Alex hadn't spoken to her for the last two days, not since the business at the tunnel. Nor had she spoken to him. He had rejected her, and he knew she would never forgive him. She hadn't come down to breakfast this morning, and he'd assumed she wouldn't show herself again until he'd gone. So what was she doing here now?

Suddenly Alex knew. She'd come to cause trouble —one last jab below the belt. He could see it in her eyes and in the way she flounced across the lawn with her hands rolled into fists.

Fiona didn't know he was a spy. But she must know that he was here for a reason, and she had probably guessed it had something to do with the woman from Point Blanc. So she had decided to come out and spoil things for him. Maybe she was going to ask questions. Maybe she was going to give Mrs. Stellenbosch a piece of her mind. Either way, Alex knew that his mission would be over before it had even begun. All his work memorizing the files and all the time he had spent with the family would have been for nothing.

"Fiona . . . ," Sir David muttered. His eyes were grave. He had come to the same conclusion as Alex.

She ignored him. "Are you from the academy?" she asked, speaking directly to Mrs. Stellenbosch.

"Yes, my dear."

"Well, I think there's something you should know."

There was only one thing Alex could do. He lifted the Harry Potter book and pointed it at Fiona, then pressed the spine once, hard. There was no noise, but he felt the book shudder in his hand. Fiona put her hand to the side of her leg. All the color drained out of her face. She crumpled to the grass.

Lady Caroline ran to her. Mrs. Stellenbosch looked puzzled. Alex turned to her, his face blank. "That's my sister," he said. "She gets very emotional."

Two minutes later, the helicopter took off. Alex watched through the window as Haverstock Hall got smaller and smaller and then disappeared behind them. He looked at Mrs. Stellenbosch, hunched over the controls, her eyes hidden by her goggles. He eased himself into his chair and let himself be carried away into the darkening sky. Then the clouds rolled in. The countryside was gone. So was his only weapon. Alex was on his own.

8
ROOM 13

IT WAS RAINING IN PARIS. The city looked tired and disappointed, the Eiffel Tower fighting against a mass of heavy clouds. There was nobody sitting at the tables outside the cafés, and for once the little kiosks selling paintings and postcards were being ignored by the tourists, who were hurrying back to their hotels. It was five o'clock in the afternoon and the evening was drawing in, unnoticed. The shops and offices were emptying, but the city didn't care. It just wanted to be left alone.

The helicopter had landed in a private area of Charles de Gaulle airport, and a car had been waiting to drive them in. Alex had said nothing during the flight and now he sat on his own in the back, watching the buildings flash by. They were following the Seine, moving surprisingly fast along a wide, two-lane road that dipped above and below the water level. Their route took them past Notre Dame. Then they turned off, weaving their way through a series of back streets with smaller restaurants and boutiques fighting for space on the pavements.

"The Marais," Mrs. Stellenbosch said to Alex, pointing out the window.

He pretended to show no interest. In fact, he had stayed in the Marais once with his uncle and knew it as one of the most sophisticated and expensive sections in Paris.

The car turned into a large square and stopped. Alex glanced out the window. He was surrounded on four sides by the tall, classical houses for which Paris is famous. But the square had been disfigured by a single modern hotel. It was a white, rectangular block, the windows fitted with dark glass that allowed no view inside. It rose up four floors with a flat roof and the name HOTEL DU MONDE in gold letters above the main door. If a spaceship had landed in the square, crushing a couple of buildings to make room for itself, it couldn't have looked more out of place.

"This is where we're staying," Mrs. Stellenbosch said. "The hotel is owned by the academy."

The driver took their cases out of the trunk. Alex followed the assistant director toward the entrance, the door sliding open automatically to allow them in. The lobby was cold and faceless, white marble and mirrors with a single potted plant tucked into a corner as an afterthought. There was a small reception desk with an unsmiling male receptionist in a dark suit and glasses, a computer, and a row of pigeonholes. Alex counted them. There were fifteen. Presumably, the hotel had fifteen rooms.

"*Bonsoir,* Madame Stellenbosch." The receptionist nodded his head slightly. He ignored Alex. "I hope you had a good journey from England," he continued, still speaking in French. Alex gazed blankly, as if he hadn't understood a word. Alex Friend wouldn't speak French. He wouldn't have bothered to learn. But Ian Rider had made certain that his nephew was speaking French almost as soon as he was speaking English. Not to mention German and Spanish as well.

The receptionist took down two keys. He didn't ask either of them to sign in. He didn't ask for a credit card. The school owned the hotel, so there would be no bill when they left. He gave Alex one of the keys.

"I hope you're not superstitious," he said, speaking in English now.

"No," Alex replied.

"It is room thirteen. On the first floor. I am sure you will find it most agreeable." The receptionist smiled.

Mrs. Stellenbosch took her key. "The hotel has its own restaurant," she said. Her voice was gravelly and strangely masculine. Her breath smelled of cigar smoke. "We might as well eat here tonight. We don't want to go out in the rain. Anyway, the food here is excellent. Do you like French food, Alex?"

"Not much," Alex said.

"Well, I'm sure we'll find something that you like. Why don't you freshen up after the journey?" She looked at her watch. "We'll eat at seven—an hour and a half from now. It will give us an opportunity to talk together. Might I suggest, perhaps, some neater clothes for dinner? The French are informal, but—if you'll forgive me saying so, my dear—you take informality a little far. I'll call you at five to seven. I hope the room is all right."

Room 13 was at the end of a long, narrow corridor. The door opened into a surprisingly large space, with views over the square. There was a double bed with a black-and-white comforter, a television and minibar, a desk, and, on the wall, a couple of framed pictures of Paris. A porter had carried up Alex's suitcase, and as soon as he was gone, Alex kicked off his shoes and sat down on the bed. He wondered why they had come here. He knew the helicopter had needed refueling, but that shouldn't have necessitated an overnight stop. Why not fly on straight to the school?

He had more than an hour to kill. First he went into the bathroom—more glass and white marble—and took a long shower. Then, wrapped in a towel, he went back into the room and turned on the television. Alex Friend would watch a lot of television. There were about thirty channels to choose from. Alex skipped past the French ones and stopped on MTV. He wondered if he was being monitored. There was a large mirror next to the desk, and it would be easy enough to conceal a camera behind it. Well, why not give them something to think about? He opened the minibar and poured himself a glass of gin. Then he went into the bathroom, refilled the bottle with water, and put it back in the fridge. Drinking alcohol and stealing! If she was watching, Madame Stellenbosch would know that she had her hands full with him.

He spent the next forty minutes watching television and pretending to drink the gin. Then he took the glass into the bathroom and dumped it in the sink. It was time to get dressed. Should he do what he was told and

put on neater clothes? In the end, he compromised.
He put on a new shirt, but kept the same jeans. A moment later, the telephone rang. His call for dinner.

Mrs. Stellenbosch was waiting for him in the
restaurant, a large, airless room in the basement. Soft
lighting and mirrors had been used to make it feel
more spacious, but it was still the last place Alex
would have chosen. The restaurant could have been
anywhere, in any part of the world. There were two
other diners—businessmen, from the looks of
them—but otherwise they were alone. Mrs. Stellenbosch had changed into a black evening dress with
feathers at the collar, and she had an antique necklace
of black and silver beads. The fancier her clothes, Alex
thought, the uglier she looked. She was smoking another cigar.

"Ah, Alex!" She blew smoke. "Did you have a rest?
Or did you watch TV?"

Alex didn't say anything. He sat down and opened
the menu, then closed it again when he saw that it was
all in French.

"You must let me order for you. Some soup to
start, perhaps? And then a steak. I've never yet met a
boy who doesn't like steak."

"My cousin Oliver is a vegetarian," Alex said. It was something he had read in one of the files.

The assistant director nodded as if she already knew this. "Then he doesn't know what he is missing," she said. A pale-faced waiter came over and she placed the order in French. "What will you drink?" she asked.

"I'll have a Coke."

"A repulsive drink, I've always thought. I have never understood the taste. But of course, you shall have what you want."

The waiter brought a Coke for Alex and a glass of champagne for Mrs. Stellenbosch. Alex watched the bubbles rising in the two glasses, his black, hers a pale yellow.

"*Santé,*" she said.

"I'm sorry?"

"It's French for good health."

"Oh. Cheers . . ."

There was a moment's silence. The woman's eyes were fixed on him as if she could see right through him. "So you were at Eton," she said casually.

"That's right." Alex was suddenly on his guard.

"What house were you in?"

"The Hopgarden." It was the name of a real house at the school. Alex had read the file carefully.

"I visited Eton once. I remember a statue. I think it was of a king. It was just through the main gate . . ."

She was testing him. Alex was sure of it. Did she suspect him? Or was it simply a precaution, something she always did? "You're talking about Henry the Sixth," he said. "His statue's in College Yard. He founded Eton."

"But you didn't like it there."

"No."

"Why not?"

"I didn't like the uniform and I didn't like the beaks." Alex was careful not to use the word *teachers*. At Eton, they're known as beaks. He half smiled to himself. If she wanted a bit of Eton-speak, he'd give it to her. "And I didn't like the rules. Getting fined by the Pop. Or being put in the Tardy Book. I was always getting Rips and Infoes . . . or being put on the Bill. The divs were boring . . ."

"I'm afraid I don't really understand a word you're saying."

"Divs are lessons," Alex explained. "Rips are when your work is no good."

"I see!" She drew a line with her cigar. "Is that why you set fire to the library?"

"No," Alex said. "That was just because I don't like books."

The first course arrived. Alex's soup was yellow and had something floating in it. He picked up his spoon and poked at it suspiciously. "What's this?" he demanded.

"Soupe de moules."

He looked at her blankly.

"Mussel soup. I hope you enjoy it."

"I'd have preferred tomato," Alex said.

The steaks, when they came, were typically French: barely cooked at all. Alex took a couple of mouthfuls of the bloody meat, then threw down his knife and fork and used his fingers to eat all the french fries. Mrs. Stellenbosch talked to him about the French Alps, about skiing, and about her visits to various European cities. It was easy to look bored. He *was* bored. And he was beginning to feel tired. He took a sip of Coke, hoping the cold drink would wake him up. The meal seemed to be dragging on all night.

But at last the desserts—ice cream with white

chocolate sauce—had come and gone. Alex declined coffee.

"You're looking tired," Mrs. Stellenbosch said. She lit another cigar. The smoke curled around her head and made him feel dizzy. "Would you like to go to bed?"

"Yes."

"We don't need to leave until midday tomorrow. You'll have time for a visit to the Louvre, if you'd like that."

Alex shook his head. "Actually, paintings bore me."

"Really? What a shame!"

Alex stood up. Somehow his hand knocked into his glass, spilling the rest of the Coke over the pristine white tablecloth. What was the matter with him? Suddenly he was exhausted.

"Would you like me to come up with you, Alex?" the woman asked. She was looking carefully at him, a tiny glimmer of interest in her otherwise dead eyes.

"No. I'll be all right." Alex stepped away. "Good night."

Getting upstairs was an ordeal. He was tempted to take the elevator, but he didn't want to lock himself into that small, windowless cubicle. He would have felt suffocated. He climbed the stairs, his shoulders resting heavily against the wall. Then he stumbled down the corridor and somehow got his key into the lock. When he finally got inside, the room was spinning. What was going on? Had he drunk more of the gin than he had intended, or was he . . . ?

Alex swallowed. He had been drugged. There had been something in the Coke. It was still on his tongue, a sort of bitterness. There were only three steps between him and his bed, but it could have been a mile away. His legs wouldn't obey him anymore. Just lifting one foot took all his strength. He fell forward, reaching out with his arms. Somehow he managed to propel himself far enough. His chest and shoulders hit the bed, sinking into the mattress. The room was spinning around him, faster and faster. He tried to stand up, tried to speak—but nothing came. His eyes closed. Gratefully, he allowed the darkness to take him.

Thirty minutes later, there was a soft click and the room began to change.

If Alex had been able to open his eyes, he would have seen the desk, the minibar, and the framed pictures of Paris begin to rise up the wall. Or so it might have seemed to him. But in fact the walls weren't moving. It was the floor that was sinking downward on hidden hydraulics, taking the bed—with Alex on it—into the depths of the hotel. The entire room was nothing more than a huge elevator that carried him, one inch at a time, into the basement and beyond.

Now the walls were metal sheets. He had left the wallpaper, the lights, and the pictures high above him. He was dropping through what might have been a ventilation shaft with four steel rods guiding him to the bottom. Brilliant lights suddenly flooded over him. There was a soft click. He had arrived.

The bed had come to rest in the center of a gleaming underground clinic. Scientific equipment crowded in on him from all sides. There were a number of cameras: digital, video, infrared, and X-ray. There were instruments of all shapes and sizes, most of them unrecognizable to anyone without a science degree. A tangle of wires spiraled out from each machine to a bank of computers that hummed and blinked on a long worktable against one of the walls. A glass window had been cut into the wall on the other side. The room was air-conditioned. Had Alex been awake, he might have shivered in the cold. His breath appeared as a faint white cloud, hovering around his mouth.

A plump man wearing a white coat had been waiting to receive him. The man, who was about forty, had yellow hair that he wore slicked back, and a face that was rapidly sinking into middle age, with puffy cheeks and a thick, fatty neck. The man had glasses and a small mustache. Two assistants were with him, also wearing white coats. Their faces were blank.

The three of them set to work at once. Handling Alex as if he were a sack of vegetables—or a corpse— they picked him up and stripped off all his clothes. Then they began to photograph him, beginning with a conventional camera. Starting at his toes, they moved upward, clicking off at least a hundred pictures, the flash igniting and the film automatically advancing. Not one inch of his body escaped their examination. A lock of his hair was snipped off and put into a plastic envelope. An opthalmoscope was used to produce a perfect image of the back of his eye. They made a mold of his teeth, slipping a piece of putty into his mouth and manipulating his chin to make him bite down. They made a careful note of the birthmark on his left shoulder, the scar on his arm, and even the ends of his fingers. Alex bit his nails; that was recorded too. Finally, they weighed him on a large, flat scale and then measured him—his height,

chest size, waist, inside leg, hand size, and so on—
making a note in their books of every measurement.

And all the time, Mrs. Stellenbosch watched from
the other side of the window. She never moved. The
only sign of life anywhere in her face was the cigar,
clamped between her lips. It glowed red, and the
smoke trickled up.

The three men had finished. The one with the yellow hair spoke into a microphone. "We're all finished," he said.

"Give me your opinion, Mr. Baxter." The
woman's voice echoed out of a speaker concealed behind the wall.

"It's a cinch." The man called Baxter was English.
He spoke with an upper-class accent, and he was obviously pleased with himself. "He's got a good bone
structure. Very fit. Interesting face. You notice the
pierced ear? He's had that done recently. Nothing else
to say, really."

"When will you operate?"

"Whenever you say, old girl. Just let me know."

Mrs. Stellenbosch turned to the other two men.
"Envoyez lui!" She snapped the two words.

The two assistants put Alex's clothes back on him.
This took longer than taking them off. As they

worked, they made a careful note of all the brand names. The Quiksilver T-shirt. The Gap socks. By the time they had dressed him, they knew as much about him as a doctor knows about a newborn baby. It had all been noted down.

Mr. Baxter walked over to the worktable and pressed a button. At once, the carpet, bed, and hotel furniture began to rise up. They disappeared through the ceiling and kept going. Alex slept on as he was carried back through the shaft, finally arriving in the space that he knew as room 13.

There was nothing to show what had happened. The whole experience had evaporated, as quickly as a dream.

9

MY NAME IS GRIEF

THE ACADEMY AT POINT Blanc had been built by a lunatic. For a time it had been used as an asylum. Alex remembered what Alan Blunt had told him as the helicopter began its final descent, the red and white helipad looming up to receive it. The photograph in the brochure had been artfully taken. Now that he could see the building for himself, he could only describe it as . . . crazy.

It was a jumble of towers and battlements, green sloping roofs and windows of every shape and size. Nothing fitted together properly. The overall design should have been simple enough: a circular central area with two wings. But one wing was longer than the other. The two sides didn't match. The academy was four floors high, but the windows were spaced in such a way that it was hard to tell where one floor ended and the next began. There was an internal courtyard that wasn't quite square, with a fountain that had frozen solid. Even the helipad, jutting out of the roof, was ugly and awkward, as if someone had thrown a giant Frisbee that had smashed into the brickwork and lodged in place.

Mrs. Stellenbosch flicked off the controls. "I will take you down to meet the director," she shouted over the noise of the blades. "Your luggage will be brought down later."

It was cold on the roof. Although it was almost the end of April, the snow covering the mountain still hadn't melted and everything was white for as far as the eye could see. The academy was built into the side of a steep slope. A little farther down, Alex saw a big iron tongue that started at ground level but then curved outward as the mountainside dropped away. It was a ski jump—the sort of thing he had seen at the winter Olympics. The end of the curve was at least fifty feet above the ground, and far below, Alex could make out a flat area, shaped like a horseshoe, where the jumpers were meant to land.

He was staring at it, imagining what it would be like to propel yourself into space with only two skis to break your fall, when the woman grabbed his arm. "We don't use it," she said. "It is forbidden. Come now! Let's get out of the cold."

They went through a door in the side of one of the towers and down a narrow spiral staircase (each step a different distance apart) that took them all the way to the ground floor. Now they were in a long, narrow corridor with plenty of doors but no windows.

"Classrooms," Mrs. Stellenbosch explained. "You will see them later."

Alex followed her through the strangely silent building. The central heating had been turned up high inside the academy, and the atmosphere was warm and heavy. They stopped at a pair of modern glass doors that opened into the courtyard Alex had seen from above. From the heat back into the cold again, Mrs. Stellenbosch led him through the doors and past the frozen fountain. A movement caught his eye, and Alex glanced up. This was something he hadn't noticed before. A sentry stood on one of the towers. He had a pair of binoculars around his neck and a submachine gun slung across one arm.

Armed guards? In a school? Alex had been here only a few minutes and already he was unnerved.

"Through here!" Mrs. Stellenbosch opened another door for him, and he found himself in the main reception hall of the academy. A log fire burned in a massive fireplace with two stone dragons guarding the flames. A grand staircase led upward. The hall was lit by a chandelier with at least a hundred bulbs. The walls were paneled with wood. The carpet was thick, dark red. A dozen pairs of eyes followed Alex as he followed Mrs. Stellenbosch down the next corridor. The hall was decorated with animal heads: a rhino, an antelope, a water buffalo, and, saddest of all, a lion. Alex wondered who had shot them.

They came to a single door that suggested they had come to the end of their journey. So far, Alex hadn't encountered any boys, but glancing out of the window, he saw two more guards marching slowly past, both of them cradling automatic machine guns.

Mrs. Stellenbosch knocked on the door.

"Come in!" Even with just two words, Alex caught the South African accent.

The door opened, and they went into a huge room that made no sense. Like the rest of the building, its shape was irregular, none of the walls running parallel. The ceiling was about fifty feet high with windows running the whole way and giving an impressive view of the slopes. The room was modern with soft lighting coming from units concealed in the walls. The furniture was ugly, but not as ugly as the animal heads on the walls and the zebra skin on the wood floor.

There were three chairs next to a small fireplace. One of them was gold and antique. A man was sitting in it. His head turned as Alex came in.

"Good afternoon, Alex," he said. "Please come and sit down."

Alex sauntered into the room and took one of the chairs. Mrs. Stellenbosch sat in the other.

"My name is Grief," the man continued. "Dr. Grief. I am very pleased to meet you and to have you here."

Alex stared at the man who was the director of Point Blanc, at the white-paper skin and the eyes burning behind the red eyeglasses. It was like meeting a skeleton, and for a moment he was lost for words. Then he recovered. "Nice place," he said.

"Do you think so?" There was no emotion whatsoever in Grief's voice. So far he had moved only his neck. "This building was designed in 1857 by a Frenchman who was certainly the world's worst architect. This was his only commission. When the first owners moved in, they had him shot."

"There are still quite a few people here with guns." Alex glanced out of the window as another pair of guards walked past.

"Point Blanc is unique," Dr. Grief explained. "As

you will soon discover, all the boys who have been sent here come from families of great wealth and importance. We have had the sons of emperors and industrialists. Boys like yourself. It follows that we could very easily become a target for terrorists. The guards are therefore here for your protection."

"That's very kind of you." Alex felt he was being too polite. It was time to show this man what sort of person he was meant to be. "But to be honest, I don't really want to be here myself. So if you'll just tell me how I get down into town, maybe I can get the next train home."

"There is no way down into town." Dr. Grief lifted a hand to stop Alex from interrupting. Alex glanced at his long skeletal fingers and at the eyes glinting red behind the glasses. The man moved as if every bone in his body had been broken and then put back together again. "The skiing season is over. It's too dangerous now. There is only the helicopter, and that will take you from here only when I say so." The hand lowered itself again. "You are here, Alex, because you have disappointed your parents. You were expelled from school. You have had difficulties with the police."

"That wasn't my bloody fault!" Alex protested.

"Don't interrupt the doctor!" Mrs. Stellenbosch said.

Alex glanced at her balefully.

"Your appearance is displeasing," Dr. Grief went on. "Your language also. It is our job to turn you into a boy of whom your parents can be proud."

"I'm happy as I am," Alex said.

"That is of no relevance." Dr. Grief fell silent.

Alex shivered. There was something about this room, so big, so empty, so twisted out of shape. And this man who was both old and young at the same time but who somehow wasn't completely human. "So what are you going to do with me?" Alex asked.

"There will be no lessons to begin with," Mrs. Stellenbosch said. "For the first couple of weeks we want you to assimilate."

"What does that mean?"

"To assimilate. To conform . . . to adapt . . . to become like." It was as if she were reading out of a dictionary. "There are six boys at the academy at the moment. You will meet them and you will spend time with them. There will be opportunities for sports and for being social. There is a good library here, and you will read. Soon you will learn our methods."

"I want to call my mom and dad," Alex said.

"The use of telephones is forbidden," Mrs. Stellenbosch explained. She tried to smile sympathetically, but with her face it wasn't quite possible. "We find it makes our students homesick," she went on. "Of course, you may write letters if you wish."

"I prefer e-mail," Alex said.

"For the same reason, e-mail is not permitted."

Alex shrugged and swore under his breath.

Dr. Grief had seen him. "You will be polite to the assistant director," he snapped. He hadn't raised his voice, but the words had an acid tone. "You should be aware, Alex, that Mrs. Stellenbosch has worked with me now for twenty-six years and that when I met her she had been voted Miss South Africa five years in a row."

Alex glanced at the hostile face. "A beauty contest?" he asked.

"The weight-lifting championships." Dr. Grief glanced at the fireplace. "Show him," he said.

Mrs. Stellenbosch got up and went over to the fireplace. There was a poker lying in the grate. She took it with both hands. For a moment she seemed to concentrate. Alex gasped. The solid metal poker, almost two inches thick, was slowly bending. Now it was U-shaped. Mrs. Stellenbosch wasn't even sweating. She brought the two ends together and dropped it back into the grate. It clanged against the stone.

"We enforce strict discipline here at the academy," Dr. Grief said. "Bedtime is at ten o'clock—not a minute past. We do not tolerate bad language. You will have no contact with the outside world without our permission. You will not attempt to leave. And you will do as you are told instantly, without hesitation. And finally . . ." He leaned toward Alex. "You are permitted only in certain parts of this building." He gestured with a hand, and for the first time Alex noticed a second door at the far end of the room. "My private quarters are through there. You will remain on the first and second floors only. That is where the bedrooms and classrooms are located. The third and fourth floors are out of bounds. The basement also. This again is for your safety."

"You're afraid I'll trip on the stairs?" Alex asked.

Dr. Grief ignored him. "You may leave," he said.

"Wait outside the office, Alex," Mrs. Stellenbosch said. "Someone will be along to get you."

Alex stood up.

"We will make you into what your parents want," Dr. Grief said.

"Maybe they don't want me at all."

"We can arrange that too."

Alex left.

"An unpleasant boy . . . a few days . . . faster than usual . . . the Gemini Project . . . closing down . . ."

If the door hadn't been so thick, Alex would have been able to hear more. The moment he had left the room he had cupped his ear against the keyhole, hoping to pick up something that might be useful to MI6. Sure enough, Dr. Grief and Mrs. Stellenbosch were busily talking on the other side, but Alex heard little and understood less.

A hand clamped down on his shoulder and he twisted around, annoyed with himself. A so-called spy caught listening at keyholes! But it wasn't one of the guards. Alex found himself looking up at a round-faced boy with long, dark hair, dark blue eyes, and pale skin. He was wearing a very old *Star Wars* T-shirt, torn jeans, and a baseball cap. Recently he had been in a fight, and it looked like he'd gotten the worst of it. There was a bruise around one of his eyes and a gash on his lip.

"They'll shoot you if they catch you listening at doors," the boy said. He looked at Alex with hostile eyes. Alex guessed that he was the sort of boy who wouldn't trust anyone easily. "I'm James Sprintz," he said. "They told me to show you around."

"Alex Friend."

"So what did you do to get sent to this dump?" James asked as they walked down the corridor.

"I got expelled from Eton."

"I got thrown out of a school in Dusseldorf." James sighed. "I thought it was the best thing that ever happened to me. Until my dad sent me here."

"What does your dad do?" Alex asked.

"He's a banker. He plays the money markets. He loves money and he has lots of it." James's voice was flat and unemotional.

"Dieter Sprintz?" Alex remembered the name. He'd made the front page of every newspaper in England a few years before. The hundred-million-dollar man. That was how much he had made in just twenty-four hours. At the same time, the pound had crashed and the British government had almost collapsed.

"Yeah. Don't ask me to show you a photograph, because I don't have one. This way . . ."

They had reached the main hall with the dragon fireplace. From here, James showed him into the dining room, a long, high-ceilinged room with six tables and a window leading into the kitchen. After that, they visited two living rooms, a games room, and a library. The academy reminded Alex of a ski resort—and not just because of its setting. There was a sort of heaviness about the place, a sense of being cut off from the real world. The air was warm and silent, and despite the size of the rooms, Alex couldn't help feeling claustrophobic. Grief had said that there were only six boys currently at the school. The building could have housed sixty. Empty space was everywhere.

There was nobody in either of the living rooms—just a collection of armchairs, desks, and tables—but they found a couple of boys in the library. This was a long, narrow room with old-fashioned oak shelves lined with books in a variety of languages. A suit of medieval Swiss armor stood in an alcove at the far end.

"This is Tom. And Hugo," James said. "They're probably doing extra math or something, so we'd better not disturb them."

The two boys looked up and nodded briefly. One of them was reading a textbook. The other had been writing. They were both much better dressed than James and didn't look very friendly.

"Creeps," James said as soon as they had left the room.

"In what way?"

"When I was told about this place, they said all the kids had problems. I thought it was going to be wild. Do you have a cigarette?"

"I don't smoke."

"Great, another one. . . . I get here and it's like a museum or a monastery or . . . I don't know what. It looks like Dr. Grief's been busy. Everyone's quiet, hardworking, boring. God knows how he did it. Sucked their brains out with a straw or something. A couple of weeks ago I got into a fight with a couple of them, just for the hell of it." He pointed to his face. "They beat the crap out of me and then went back to their studies. Really creepy!"

They went into the games room, which contained table tennis, darts, a wide-screen TV, and a snooker table. "Don't try playing snooker," James said. "The room's on a slant and all the balls roll the wrong way."

Then they went upstairs, where the boys had their study-bedrooms. Each one contained a bed, an armchair, a television ("It shows only the programs Dr. Grief wants you to see," James said), a bureau, and a desk. A second door led into a small bathroom with a toilet and shower. None of the rooms was locked.

"We're not allowed to lock them," James explained. "We're all stuck here with nowhere to go, so nobody bothers to steal anything. I heard that Hugo Vries—the boy in the library—used to steal anything he could get his hands on. He was arrested for shoplifting in Amsterdam."

"But not anymore?"

"He's another success story. He's flying home next week. His father owns diamond mines. Why bother shoplifting when you can afford to buy the whole shop?"

Alex's study was at the end of the corridor, with views over the ski jump. His suitcases had already been carried up and were waiting for him on the bed. Everything felt very bare, but according to James, the study-bedrooms were the only part of the school the boys were allowed to decorate themselves. They could choose their own bedspreads and cover the walls with their own posters.

"They say it's important that you express yourself," James said. "If you haven't brought anything with you, Miss Stomach-bag will take you into Grenoble."

"Stomach-bag?"

"Mrs. Stellenbosch. That's my name for her."

"What do the other boys call her?"

"They call her Mrs. Stellenbosch." James sighed. "I'm telling you—this is a deeply weird place, Alex. I've been to a lot of schools because I've been thrown out of a lot of schools. But this one is the pits. I've been here for six weeks now and I've hardly had any lessons. They have music evenings and discussion evenings and they try to get me to read. But otherwise, I've been left on my own."

"They want you to assimilate," Alex said, remembering what Dr. Grief had said.

"That's their word for it. But this place . . . they may call it a school, but it's more like being in prison. You've seen the guards."

"I thought they were here to protect us."

"If you think that, you're a bigger idiot than I thought. Think about it! There are about thirty of them. Thirty armed guards for seven kids? That's not protection. That's intimidation." James paused by the door. He examined Alex for a second time. "It would be nice to think that someone has finally arrived who I can relate to," he said.

"Maybe you can," Alex said.

"Yeah. But for how long?"

James left, closing the door behind him.

Alex began to unpack. The bulletproof ski suit and

infrared goggles were at the top of the first suitcase. It didn't look as if he would be needing them. It wasn't as if he even had any skis. Then came the Discman. He remembered the instructions Smithers had given him. *"If you're in real trouble, just press FAST FORWARD three times."* He was almost tempted to do it now. There was something unsettling about the academy. He could feel it even now, in his room. He was like a goldfish in a bowl. Looking up, he almost expected to see a pair of huge eyes looming over him, and he knew that they would be wearing red-tinted glasses. He weighed the Discman in his hand. He couldn't hit the panic button—yet. He had nothing to report back to MI6. There was nothing to connect the school with the deaths of the two men in New York and the Black Sea.

But if there was anything, he knew where he would find it. Why were two whole floors of the building out of bounds? It made no sense at all. Presumably the guards slept up there, but even though Dr. Grief seemed to employ a small army, that would still leave a lot of empty rooms. The third and fourth floors. If something was going on at the academy, it had to be going on up there.

A bell sounded downstairs. Alex shut his suitcase,

left his room, and walked down the corridor. He saw another couple of boys walking ahead of him, talking quietly together. Like the boys he had seen in the library, they were clean and well dressed with hair cut short and neatly groomed. Really creepy, James had said. Even on first sight, Alex had to agree.

He reached the main staircase. The two boys had gone down. Alex glanced in their direction, then went up. The staircase turned a corner and stopped. Ahead of him was a sheet of metal that rose up from the floor to the ceiling and all the way across, blocking off the view. The wall had been added recently, like the helipad. Someone had carefully and deliberately cut the building in two.

There was a door set in the metal wall and beside it a keypad with nine buttons demanding a code. Alex reached for the door handle, his hand closing around it. He didn't expect the door to open—nor did he expect what happened next. The moment his fingers came into contact with the handle, an alarm went off, a shrieking siren that echoed throughout the building. A few seconds later, he heard footsteps on the stairs and turned to find two guards facing him, their guns half raised.

Neither of them spoke. One of them ran past him

and punched a code into the keypad. The alarm stopped. And then Mrs. Stellenbosch was there, hurrying forward on her short, muscular legs.

"Alex!" she exclaimed. Her eyes were filled with suspicion. "What are you doing here? The director told you that the upper floors are forbidden."

"Yeah . . . well, I forgot." Alex looked straight at her. "I heard the bell go and I was on my way to the dining room."

"The dining room is downstairs."

"Right."

Alex walked past the two guards, who stepped aside to let him pass. He felt Mrs. Stellenbosch watching him while he went. Metal doors, alarms, and guards with machine guns. What were they trying to hide? And then he remembered something else. The Gemini Project. Those were the words he had heard when he was listening at Dr. Grief's door.

Gemini. The twins. One of the twelve star signs.

But what did it mean?

Turning the question over his mind, Alex went down to meet the rest of the students.

10

THINGS THAT GO CLICK IN THE NIGHT

AT THE END OF HIS FIRST week at Point Blanc, Alex drew up a list of the six boys with whom he shared the school. It was midafternoon, and he was alone in his room. A notepad was open in front of him. It had taken him about half an hour to put together the names and the few details that he had. He only wished he had more.

HUGO VRIES (14) Dutch. Lives in Amsterdam. Brown hair, green eyes. Father's name, Rudi. Owns diamond mines. Speaks little English. Reads and plays guitar. Very solitary. Sent to PB for major shoplifting and arson.

TOM MCMORIN (14) Canadian. From Vancouver. Parents divorced. Mother runs media empire (newspapers, TV). Reddish hair, blue eyes. Well built, chess player. Car thefts and drunken driving . . . sent to PB.

NICOLAS MARC (14) French . . . from Bordeaux? Expelled from private school in Paris, cause unknown. Drugs? Brown hair, brown eyes, very fit all around. Tattoo of devil on left shoulder. Good at sports. Father = Anthony Marc. Airlines, pop music, hotels. Never mentions his mother.

CASSIAN JAMES (14) American. Fair hair, brown eyes. Mother = Jill . . . studio chief in Hollywood. Parents divorced. Writes poetry, plays jazz piano. Expelled from six schools. Various drugs offenses. Sent to PB after smuggling arrest. Tells jokes. Seems popular.

JOE CANTERBURY (14) American. Spends much of his time with Cassian. Brown hair, blue eyes. Mother (name unknown) New York senator. Father something major at the Pentagon. Vandalism, truancy, shoplifting. Claims to have own motorbike and three girlfriends (!) in Los Angeles.

JAMES SPRINTZ (14) German. Father = Dieter Sprintz, banker, well-known financier (the hundred-million-dollar man). Mother living in England. Brown hair, dark blue eyes, pale. Lives in Dusseldorf. Expelled for wounding a teacher with an air pistol. Closest I've got to a friend at PB—the only one who really hates it here.

Lying on his bed, Alex studied the list. What did it tell him? Not a great deal.

First, all the boys were the same age: fourteen, the same age as him. At least three of them, and possibly four, had parents who were either divorced or separated. They all came from hugely wealthy backgrounds. Blunt had already told him that was the case, but Alex was surprised by just how diverse the parents were. Airlines, diamonds, politics, and movies. France, Holland, Canada, and America. Each one of them was at the top of his or her field, and those fields covered just about every human activity. He himself was supposed to be the son of a supermarket king. Food. That was another world industry he could check off.

At least two of the boys had been arrested for shoplifting. Two had been involved with drugs. But Alex knew that the list somehow hid more than it revealed. With the exception of James, it was hard to pin down what made the boys at Point Blanc different. In a strange way, they all looked the same.

Their eyes and hair were different colors. They wore different clothes. All the faces were different: Tom handsome and confident, Joe quiet and watchful. And of course they spoke not only with different voices but also in several languages. James had talked about brains being sucked out with straws, and he had a point. It was as if the same consciousness had somehow invaded them all. They had become puppets, dancing on the same string.

The bell rang downstairs. Alex looked at his watch. It was exactly one o'clock—lunchtime. That was another thing about the school. Everything was done to the exact minute. Lessons from nine until twelve. Lunch from one to two. And so on. James made a point of being late for everything, and Alex had taken to joining him. It was a tiny rebellion but a satisfying one. It showed they still had a little control over their own lives. The other boys, of course, turned up like clockwork. They would be in the dining room now, waiting quietly for the food to be served.

Alex rolled over on the bed and reached for a pen. He wrote a single word on the pad, underneath the names.

BRAINWASHING?

Maybe that was the answer. According to James, the other boys had arrived at the academy two months before him. He had been there for just three weeks.

That added up to just eleven weeks in total, and Alex knew that you didn't take a bunch of delinquents and turn them into perfect students just by giving them good books. Dr. Grief had to be doing something else. Drugs. Hypnosis. Something.

He waited five more minutes, then hid the notepad under his mattress and left the room. He wished he could lock the door. There was no privacy at Point Blanc. Even the bathrooms had no locks. And Alex still couldn't shake off the feeling that everything he did, even everything he thought, was somehow being monitored, noted down. Evidence to be used against him.

It was ten past one when he reached the dining room, and sure enough, the other boys were already there, eating their lunch and talking quietly among themselves. Nicolas and Cassian were at one table. Hugo, Tom, and Joe were at another. Nobody was flicking peas. Nobody even had their elbows on the table. Tom was talking about a visit he had made to some museum in Grenoble. Alex had been in the room only a few seconds, but already his appetite had gone.

James had arrived just ahead of him and was standing at one of the windows into the kitchen, helping himself to food. Most of the food arrived

precooked, and one of the guards heated it up. Today
it was stew. Alex got his lunch and sat next to James.
The two of them had their own table. They had become friends quite effortlessly. Everyone else ignored
them.

"You want to go out after lunch?" James asked.

"Sure. Why not?"

"There's something I want to talk to you about."

Alex looked past James at the other boys. There
was Tom, at the head of the table, reaching out for a
pitcher of water. He was dressed in a polo shirt and
jeans. Next to him was Joe Canterbury. He was talking to Hugo now, waving a finger to emphasize a
point. Where had Alex seen that movement before?
Cassian was just behind them, round faced, with fine,
light brown hair, laughing at a joke.

Different but the same. Watching them closely,
Alex tried to figure out what he meant.

It was all in the details, the things you wouldn't
notice unless you saw them all together, like they were
now. The way they were all sitting with their backs
straight and their elbows close to their sides. The way
they held their knives and forks. Hugo laughed, and
Alex realized that for a moment he had become a mirror image of Cassian. It was the same laugh. He

watched Joe eat a mouthful of food. Then he watched Nicolas. They were two different boys. There was no doubting that. But they ate in the same way, as if mimicking each other.

There was a movement at the door, and suddenly Mrs. Stellenbosch appeared. "Good afternoon, boys," she said.

"Good afternoon, Mrs. Stellenbosch." Five people answered, but Alex heard only one voice. He and James had remained silent.

"Lessons this afternoon will begin at three o'clock. The subjects will be Latin and French."

The lessons were taught by Dr. Grief or Mrs. Stellenbosch. There were no other teachers at the school. Alex hadn't yet been taught anything. James dipped in and out of class, depending on his mood.

"There will be a discussion this evening in the library," Mrs. Stellenbosch went on. "The subject is violence in television and film. Tom, you will open the debate. Afterward, there will be hot chocolate, and Dr. Grief will give a lecture on the works of Mozart. Everyone is welcome to attend."

James jabbed a finger into his open mouth and stuck out his tongue. Alex smiled. The other boys were listening quietly.

"Dr. Grief would also like to congratulate Cassian James on winning the poetry competition. His poem is pinned to the bulletin board in the main hall. That is all."

She turned and left the room. James rolled his eyes. "Let's go out and get some fresh air," he said. "I'm feeling sick."

The two of them went upstairs and put on their coats. James had the room next door to Alex and had done his best to make it more homey. There were posters of old sci-fi movies on the wall and a mobile with the solar system dangling above the bed. A lava lamp bubbled and swirled on the bedside table, casting an orange glow. There were clothes everywhere. James obviously didn't believe in hanging them up. Somehow he managed to find a scarf and a single glove. He shoved one hand into a pocket. "Let's go," he said.

They went back down and along the corridor, passing the games room. Nicolas and Cassian were playing table tennis, and Alex stopped at the door to watch them. The ball was bouncing back and forth, and Alex found himself mesmerized. He stood there for about sixty seconds, watching. Kerplink, kerplunk, kerplink, kerplunk—neither of the boys was scoring.

There it was again. Different but the same. Obviously, there were two boys there. But the way they played, the style of their game, was identical. If it had been one boy knocking a ball against a mirror, the result would have looked much the same. Alex shivered. James was standing at his shoulder. The two of them moved away.

Hugo was sitting in the library. The boy who had been sent to Point Blanc for shoplifting was reading a Dutch edition of *National Geographic* magazine. They reached the hall, and there was Cassian's poem, prominently pinned to the bulletin board. He had been sent to Point Blanc for smuggling drugs. Now he was writing about daffodils.

Alex pushed open the main door and felt the cold wind hit his face. He was grateful for it. He needed to be reminded that there was a real world outside this bizarre goldfish bowl.

It had begun to snow again. The two boys walked slowly around the building. A couple of guards walked toward them, speaking softly in German. Alex had counted thirty guards at Point Blanc, all of them young German men, dressed in uniform black roll-neck sweaters and black vests. The guards never spoke to the boys. They had the pale, unhealthy faces and close-cropped hair he would have expected. Dr. Grief had said they were there for his protection, but Alex still wondered. Were they here to keep intruders out, or the boys in?

"This way," James said.

James walked ahead, his feet sinking into the thick snow. Alex followed, looking back at the windows on the third and fourth floors. It was maddening. A whole half of the castle—perhaps more—was closed off to him, and he still couldn't think of a way of getting up to it. He couldn't climb. The brickwork was too smooth and there was no convenient ivy to provide handholds. The drainpipes looked too fragile to take his weight.

Something moved. Alex stopped in his tracks.

"What is it?" James asked.

"There!" Alex pointed at the third floor. He thought he'd seen a figure, watching them from behind the window directly above his room. It was there for only a moment. The face seemed to be masked. A white mask with a narrow slit for the eyes. But even as he pointed, the figure stepped back, out of sight.

"I don't see anything," James said.

"It's gone."

They walked on, heading for the abandoned ski

jump. According to James, the jump had been built just before Grief had bought the academy. There had been plans to turn the building into a winter sports training center. The jump had never been used. They reached the wooden barriers that lay across the entrance and stopped.

"Let me ask you something," James said. His breath was misting in the cold air. "What do you think of this place?"

"Why do we have to talk out here?" Alex asked. Despite his coat, he was beginning to shiver.

"Because when I'm inside the building, I get the feeling that someone is listening to every word I say."

Alex nodded. "I know what you mean." He considered the question James had put to him. "I think you were right the first day we met," he said. "This place is creepy."

"So how would you feel about getting out of here?"

"You know how to fly the helicopter?"

"No. But I'm going." James paused and looked around. The two guards had gone into the school. There was nobody else in sight. "I can trust you, Alex, because you've just gotten here. He hasn't gotten to you yet." Dr. Grief. James didn't need to say the name. "But believe me," he went on, "it won't be long. If you stay here, you're going to end up like the others. Model students. That's exactly the word for them. It's like they're all made out of plastic. Well, I've had enough. I'm not going to let him do that to me."

"Are you going to run away?" Alex asked.

"Who needs to run?" James looked down the slope. "I'm going to ski."

Alex looked at the slope. It plunged steeply down, stretching on forever. "Is that possible?" he asked. "I thought—"

"I know Grief says it's too dangerous. But he would, wouldn't he? It's true that it's expert black runs all the way down, and there's bound to be tons of moguls . . ."

"Won't the snow have melted?"

"Only farther down." James pointed. "I've been right down to the bottom," he said. "I did it the first week I was here. All the slopes run into a single valley. It's called La Vallée de Fer. You can't actually make it as far as the town because there's a train track that cuts across. But if I can get to the track, I reckon I can walk the rest of the way."

"And then?"

"A train back to Dusseldorf. If my dad tries to send

me back here, I'll go to my mom in England. If she doesn't want me, I'll disappear. I've got friends in Paris and Berlin. I don't care. All I know is, I've got to split, and if you know what's good for you, you'll come too."

Alex considered. He was almost tempted to join the other boy, if only to help him on his way. But he had a job to do. "I don't have any skis," he said.

"Nor do I." James spat into the snow. "Grief took all the skis when the season ended. He's got them locked up somewhere."

"On the third floor?"

"Maybe. But I'll find them. And then I'm out of here." He reached out to Alex with his ungloved hand. "Come with me."

Alex shook his head. "I'm sorry, James. You go, and good luck to you. But I'll stick it out a bit longer. I don't want to break my neck."

"Okay. That's your choice. I'll send you a post-card."

The two of them walked back toward the school. Alex gestured at the window where he had seen the masked face. "Have you ever wondered what goes on up there?" he asked.

"No." James shrugged. "I suppose that's where the guards live."

"Two whole floors?"

"There's a basement as well. And Dr. Grief's rooms. Do you think he sleeps with Miss Stomachbag?" James made a face. "That's a pretty gross thought, the two of them together. Darth Vader and King Kong. Well, I'm going to find my skis and get out of here, Alex. And if you've got any sense, you'll come too."

Alex and James were skiing together down the slope, the blades cutting smoothly through the surface snow. It was a perfect night—everything frozen and still. They had left the academy behind them. But then Alex saw the figure ahead of them. Dr. Grief was there. He was standing motionless, wearing his dark suit, his eyes hidden by his round wire glasses. Alex veered away from him. He had lost control. He was moving faster and faster down the slope, his poles flailing at the air, his skis refusing to turn. He could see the ski jump ahead of him. Someone had removed the barriers. He felt his skis leave the snow and shoot forward onto solid ice. And then it was a screaming drop down, tearing

ever farther into the night, knowing there was no way
back. Dr. Grief laughed, and at the same moment
there was a click and Alex was shot into space, spin-
ning a mile above the ground and then falling, falling,
falling . . .

He woke up.

He was lying in bed, the moonlight spilling onto
his covers. He looked at his watch. A quarter past two.
He played back the dream he had just had. Trying to
escape with James. Dr. Grief waiting for them. He
had to admit, the academy was beginning to get to
him. He didn't usually have bad dreams. But the
school and the people in it were slipping under his
skin, working their way into his mind.

He thought about what he had heard. Dr. Grief
laughing and something else . . . a clicking sound.
That was strange. What had gone click? Had it actually been part of the dream? Suddenly, Alex was completely awake. He got out of bed, went to the door,
and turned the handle. He was right. He hadn't imagined the sound. While he was asleep, the door had
been locked from the outside.

Something had to be happening—and Alex was
determined to see what it was. He got dressed as
quickly as possible, then knelt down and examined the

lock. He could make out two bolts, at least a half inch in diameter, one at the top and one at the bottom. They must have been activated automatically. One thing was sure: he wasn't going to get out through the door.

That left the window. All the bedroom windows were fastened with a steel rod that allowed them to open ten inches but no more. Alex picked up his CD player, put in the Beethoven CD, and turned it on. The CD spun around—moving at a fantastic speed—then slowly edged forward, still spinning, until it protruded out of the casing. Alex pressed the edge of the CD against the steel rod. It took just a few seconds. The CD cut through the steel like scissors through paper. The rod fell away, allowing the window to swing fully open.

It was still snowing. Alex turned the CD player off and threw it back on his bed. Then he put on some sweats and his coat and climbed out the window. He was two floors up. Normally a fall from that height would have broken an ankle or a leg. But it had been snowing for the better part of ten hours, and a white bank had built up against the wall right beneath him. Alex lowered himself as far as he could, then let go. He fell through the air and hit the snow, disappearing as far as his waist. He felt his feet strike the hard undersoil, but the bank had protected him. He was cold and damp before he had even started. But he was unhurt.

He climbed out of the snow and began to move around the side of the building, making for the front. He would just have to hope that the main entrance wasn't locked too. But somehow he was sure it wouldn't be. His door had been locked automatically. Presumably a switch had been thrown and all the others had been locked too. Most of the boys would be asleep. Even the ones who were awake wouldn't be going anywhere, leaving Dr. Grief free to do whatever he wanted, coming and going as he pleased.

Alex had just made it to the side of the building when he heard the guards approach, boots crunching. There was nowhere to hide, so he threw himself facedown onto the snow, hugging the shadows. There were two guards. He could hear them talking softly in German, but he didn't dare look up. If he made any movement, they would see him. If they came too close, they would probably see him anyway. He held his breath, his heart pounding.

The guards walked past and rounded the corner. Their path would take them under his room. Would they see the open window? Alex had left the light off. With luck, there would be no reason for them to look up. But he was still aware that he might not have much time. He had to move—now.

He lifted himself up and ran forward. His clothes were covered in snow, and more flakes were falling, drifting into his eyes. It was the coldest part of the night, and Alex was shivering by the time he reached the main door. What would he do if it was locked after all? He certainly wouldn't be able to stay out in the open until morning.

But the door was unlocked. Alex pushed it open and slipped into the warmth and darkness of the main hall. The dragon fireplace was in front of him. There had been a fire earlier in the evening, and the burned-out logs were still smoldering in the hearth. Alex held his hands against the glow, trying to draw a little warmth into himself. Everything was silent. The empty corridors stretched into the distance, illuminated by a few low-watt bulbs that had been left on at intervals. Only now did it occur to Alex that he could have been mistaken from the start. Perhaps the doors were locked every night as part of the security. Perhaps he had jumped too quickly to the wrong conclusion and there was nothing going on at all.

"No!"

It was a boy's voice—a long, quavering shout that echoed through the school. A moment later, Alex heard feet stamping along a wooden corridor somewhere above. He looked for somewhere to hide and found it inside the fireplace, right next to the logs. The actual fire was contained in a metal basket, and there was a wide space on each side between the basket and the brickwork. Alex crouched low, feeling the heat on the side of his face and legs. He looked out, past the two dragons, waiting to see what would happen.

Three people were coming down the stairs. Mrs. Stellenbosch was the first. She was followed by two of the guards, dragging something between them. It was a boy! He was facedown, dressed only in his pajamas, his bare feet sliding down the stone steps. Mrs. Stellenbosch opened the library door and went in. The two guards followed. The door crashed shut. The silence returned.

It had all happened very quickly. Alex had been unable to see the boy's face. But he was sure he knew who it was. He had known just from the sound of his voice.

James Sprintz.

Alex eased himself out of the fireplace and crossed the hall, making for the library door. There was no sound coming from the other side. He knelt down and looked through the keyhole. No lights were on inside the room. He could see nothing. What should he do? If he went back upstairs, he could make it back to his room without being seen. He could wait until the doors were unlocked and then slip into bed. Nobody would know he had been out.

But the only person in the school who had shown him any kindness was on the other side of the library door. He had been dragged down here. Perhaps he was being brainwashed . . . beaten, even. Alex couldn't just turn around and leave him.

Alex had made his decision. He threw open the door and walked in.

The library was empty.

He stood in the doorway, blinking. The library had only one door. All the windows were closed. There were no lights on and no sign that anyone had been there. The suit of armor stood in its alcove at the end, watching him as he moved forward. Could he have been mistaken? Could Mrs. Stellenbosch and the guards have gone into a different room?

Alex went over to the alcove and looked behind the armor, wondering if there might be a second exit concealed there. There was nothing. He tapped a knuckle against the wall. Curiously, it seemed to be made of metal, but unlike the wall across the stairs, there was no handle, nothing to suggest a way through.

There was nothing more he could do here. Alex decided to go back to his room before he was discovered.

But he had just made it to the second floor when he heard voices once again . . . more guards, walking slowly down the corridor. Alex saw an empty door and slipped inside, once again ducking out of sight. He was in the laundry room. There was a washing machine, a dryer, and two ironing boards. At least it was warm in here. He felt himself surrounded by the smell of soap.

The guards walked past, and soon the sound of their footsteps disappeared. There was a second metallic click that seemed to stretch the full length of the corridor, and Alex realized that all the doors had been unlocked at the same time. He could go back to bed. He crept out and hurried forward. His footsteps took him past James Sprintz's room, next to his own.

He noticed that James's door was open. And then a voice called out from inside.

"Alex?" It was James.

No. That wasn't possible. But there was someone in his room.

Alex looked inside. The light went on.

It *was* James. He was sitting up in bed, bleary-eyed, as if he had just woken up. Alex stared at him. He was wearing the same pajamas as the boy he had just seen dragged into the library . . . but that couldn't have been him. It must have been someone else.

"What are you doing?" James asked.

"I thought I heard something," Alex said.

"But you're dressed. And you're soaking wet!" James looked at his watch. "It's almost three."

Alex was surprised that so much time had passed. It had been only a quarter past two when he had woken up. "Are you all right?" he asked.

"Yeah . . ."

"You haven't . . . ?"

"What?"

"Nothing. I'll see you tomorrow."

Alex crept back to his own room. He closed the door, then stripped off his wet clothes, dried himself with a towel, and got back into bed. If it hadn't been James he had seen being taken into the library, who was it? And yet it *had* been James; he was sure of it. He had heard the shout, seen the limp form on the stairs. So why was James lying now?

Alex closed his eyes and tried to get back to sleep. The movements of the night had created more puzzles and had solved nothing. But at least he'd gotten something out of it all.

He now knew how to get up to the third floor.

11
SEEING DOUBLE

JAMES WAS ALREADY EATING his breakfast when Alex came down: eggs, bacon, toast, and tea. He had the same breakfast every day. He raised a hand in greeting as Alex came in. But the moment he saw him, Alex got the feeling that something was wrong. James was smiling, but he seemed somehow distant, as if his thoughts were on other things.

"So what was all that about last night?" James asked.

"I don't know. . . ." Alex was tempted to tell James everything—even the fact that he was here under a false name and that he had been sent to spy on the school. But he couldn't do it. Not here, so close to the other boys. "I think I had some sort of bad dream."

"Did you go sleepwalking in the snow?"

"No. I thought I saw something, but I couldn't have. I just had a weird night." He changed the subject, lowering his voice. "Have you thought any more about your plan?" he asked.

"What plan?"

"Skiing."

"We're not allowed to ski."

"I mean . . . escaping."

James smiled as if he'd only just remembered what Alex was talking about. "Oh—I've changed my mind," he said.

"What do you mean?"

"If I ran away, my dad would only send me back again. There's no point. I might as well grin and bear it. Anyway, I'd never get all the way down the mountain. The snow's too thin."

Alex stared at James. Everything he was saying was the exact opposite of what he had said the day before. He almost wondered if this was the same boy. But of course it was. He was as untidy as ever. The bruises—fading now—were still there on his face. Dark hair, dark blue eyes, pale skin—it was James. And yet, something had happened. He was sure of it.

Then James twisted around, and Alex saw that Mrs. Stellenbosch had come into the room, wearing a particularly nasty lime green dress that came down just to her knees. "Good morning, boys!" she announced. "We're starting today's lessons in ten min-utes. The first lesson is history in the tower room." She walked over to Alex's table. "James, I hope you're going to join us today."

James shrugged. "All right, Mrs. Stellenbosch."

"Excellent. We're looking at the life of Adolf Hitler. Such an interesting man. I'm sure you'll find it most valuable." She walked away.

Alex turned to James. "You're going to class?"

"Why not?" James had finished eating. "I'm stuck here and there isn't much else to do. Maybe I should have gone to class before. You shouldn't be so nega-tive, Alex." He waved a finger to underline what he was saying. "You're wasting your time."

Alex froze. He had seen that movement before, the way he had waved his finger. Joe Canterbury, the American boy, had done exactly the same thing yes-terday.

Puppets dancing on the same string.

What had happened last night?

Alex watched James leave with the others. He felt he had lost his only friend at Point Blanc, and sud-denly he wanted to be away from this place, off the mountain and back in the safe world of Brookland Comprehensive. There might have been a time when he had wanted this adventure. Now he just wanted out of it. Press FAST FORWARD three times on his CD player and MI6 would come for him. But he couldn't do that until he had something to report.

Alex knew what he had to do. He got up and left the room.

He had seen the way the night before when he was hiding in the fireplace. The chimney bent and twisted its way to the open air. He had been able to see a chink of light from the bottom. Moonlight. The bricks outside the academy might be too smooth to climb, but inside the chimney they were broken and uneven with plenty of hand- and footholds. Maybe there would be a fireplace on the third or fourth floors. But even if there weren't, the chimney would still lead him to the roof and—assuming there weren't any guards waiting for him there—he might be able to find a way down.

Alex reached the fireplace with the two stone dragons. He looked at his watch. Ten o'clock. Classes would continue until lunch, and nobody would wonder where he was. The fire had finally gone out, although the ashes were still warm. Would one of the guards come to clean it? He would just have to hope that they would leave it until the afternoon. He looked up the chimney. He could see a narrow slit of bright blue. The sky seemed a very long way away, and the chimney was narrower than he had thought. What if he got stuck? He forced the thought out of his head, reached for a crack in the brickwork, and pulled himself up.

The inside of the chimney smelled of a thousand fires. Soot hung in the air, and Alex couldn't breathe without taking it in. He managed to find a foothold and pushed, sliding himself a short way up. Now he was wedged inside, forced into a sitting position with his feet against one wall, his back against the other, and his legs and bottom hanging in the air. He wouldn't need to use his hands at all. He only had to straighten his legs to push himself up, using the pressure of his feet against the wall to keep himself in place. Push and slide. He had to be careful. Every movement brought more soot trickling down. He could feel it in his hair. He didn't dare look up. If it went into his eyes he would be blinded. Push and slide again, then again. Not too fast. If his feet slipped he would fall all the way back down. He was already a long way above the fireplace. How far had he gone? At least one floor . . . meaning that he had to be on his way to the third. If he fell from this height, he would break both his legs.

The chimney was getting darker and tighter. The light at the top didn't seem to be getting any nearer. Alex found it difficult to maneuver himself. He could barely breathe. His entire mouth seemed to be coated in soot. He pushed again, and this time his knees banged into brickwork, sending a spasm of pain down to his feet. Pinning himself in place, Alex reached up and tried to feel where he was going. There was an L-shaped wall jutting out above his head. His knees had hit the bottom part of it. But his head was behind the upright section. Whatever the obstruction was, it effectively cut the passageway in half, leaving only the narrowest of gaps for Alex's shoulders and body to pass through.

Once again, the nightmare prospect of getting stuck flashed into his mind. Nobody would ever find him. He would suffocate in the dark. He gasped for breath and swallowed soot. One last try! He pushed again, his arms stretching out over his head. He felt his back slide up the wall, the rough brickwork tearing at his shirt. Then his hands hooked over what he realized must be the top of the *L*. He pulled himself up and found himself looking into a second fireplace, sharing the main chimney. That was the obstruction he had just climbed around. Alex raised himself over the top and dived clumsily forward. More logs and ashes broke his fall. He had made it to the third floor!

He crawled out of the fireplace. Only a few weeks before, at Brookland, he'd been reading about Victorian chimney sweeps, how boys as young as nine had been forced into virtual slave labor. He had never thought he would learn how they felt. He coughed and spat into the palm of his hand. His saliva was black. He wondered what he must look like. He would have to have a bath before he was seen.

He stood up. The third floor was as silent as the first and second. Soot trickled out of his hair, and for a moment he was blinded. He propped himself against a statue while he wiped his eyes. Then he looked again. He was leaning on a stone dragon, identical to the one on the ground floor. He looked at the fireplace. That too was identical. In fact . . .

Alex wondered if he hadn't somehow made a terrible mistake. He was standing in a hall that was the same in every detail as the hall on the ground floor. There were the same corridors, the same staircase, the same fireplace . . . even the same animal heads staring miserably from the walls. It was as if he had climbed in a circle, arriving back where he had begun. He turned around. No. Here was one difference. There was no main door. He could look down on the front courtyard from the window. There was a guard leaning against a wall, smoking a cigarette. This *was* the third floor. But it had been constructed as a perfect replica of the first.

Alex tiptoed forward, worried that somebody might have heard him climb out of the fireplace. But there was no one around. He followed the corridor as far as the first door. On the first floor, this would lead into the library. Gently, an inch at a time, he opened the door. It led into a second library—again, the spitting image of the first. It had the same tables and chairs, the same suit of armor guarding the same alcove. He ran an eye along one of the shelves. It even had the same books.

But there was one difference—at least, one difference that Alex could see. He felt as if he had strayed into one of those puzzles they sometimes printed in comics or magazines: two identical pictures, but ten deliberate mistakes. Can you spot them? The mistake here was that there was a large television set built into a shelf on a wall. The television was on. Alex found himself looking at an image of yet another library. He was beginning to feel dizzy. What was the library on the television screen? It couldn't be this one because Alex himself was not being shown. So it had to be the library on the first floor.

Two identical libraries. You could sit in one and watch the other. But why? What was the point?

It took Alex about ten minutes to discover that the entire third floor was a carbon copy of the first floor with the same dining room, living rooms, and games room. Alex went over to the snooker table and placed a ball in the middle. It rolled into the corner pocket. The room was on the same slant. A television screen showed the games room downstairs. It was the same as in the library: one room spying on another.

He retraced his steps and climbed the stairs to the fourth floor. He wanted to find his own room, but first he went into James's. It was another perfect copy: the same sci-fi posters, the same mobile hanging over the bed, the same lava lamp on the same table. There were even the same clothes strewn over the floor. So these rooms weren't just built to be the same—they were carefully maintained. Whatever happened downstairs, happened upstairs. But did that mean there had been somebody living here, watching every movement that James Sprintz made, doing everything he did? And if so, had somebody else been doing the same for him?

Alex went next door. It was like stepping into his own room. Again there was the same bed, the same furnishings, the same television. He turned it on. The picture showed his room on the first floor. There was the CD player, lying on the bed. There were his wet clothes from the night before. Had somebody been watching when he cut through the window and climbed out into the night? Alex felt a jolt of alarm, then forced himself to relax. This room—the copy of his room—was different. Nobody had moved in here yet. He could tell, just by looking around him. The bed hadn't been slept in. And the smaller details hadn't yet been copied. There was no CD player in the duplicate room. No wet clothes. He had left the closet door open downstairs. In here it was closed.

The whole thing was like some sort of mind-bending puzzle. Alex forced himself to think it through. Every single boy who arrived at the academy was watched. All his actions were duplicated. If he hung a poster on the wall of his room, an identical poster was hung in an identical room. There would be someone living in this room, doing everything that Alex did. He remembered the figure he had glimpsed the day before . . . someone wearing what looked like a white mask. Perhaps that person had been about to move in. But all the evidence suggested that, for whatever reason, he wasn't here yet.

And that still left the biggest question of all. What was the point? To spy on the boys was one thing. But to copy everything they did?

A door swung shut and he heard voices, two men walking down the corridor outside. Alex crept over to the door and looked out. He just had time to see Dr. Grief walk through a door with another man, a short, plump figure in a white coat. They had gone into the laundry room. Alex slipped out of the duplicate bedroom and followed them.

". . . you have completed the work. I am grateful to you, Mr. Baxter."

"Thank you, Dr. Grief."

They had left the door open. Alex crouched down and looked through. Here at last was a section of the third floor that didn't mirror the first. There were no washing machines or ironing boards here. Instead, Alex found himself looking into a room with a row of sinks and a second set of doors leading into a fully equipped operating room at least twice as big as the laundry room on the first floor. At the center of the room was an operating table. The walls were lined with shelves containing surgical equipment, chemicals, and—scattered across the surface—what looked like black-and-white photographs.

An operating room! What was its role in this bizarre, devilish jigsaw puzzle? The two men had walked into it and were talking together, Grief standing with one hand in his pocket. Alex chose his moment, then slipped into the outer room, crouching down beside one of the sinks. The second set of doors was open. From here he could watch and listen as the two of them talked.

"So . . . I hope you're pleased with the last operation." It was Mr. Baxter speaking. He had half turned toward the doors, and Alex could see a round, flabby face with yellow hair and a thin mustache. Baxter was wearing a bow tie and a checked suit underneath his white coat. Alex had never seen the man before. He was certain of it. And yet, he sensed he knew him. Another puzzle!

"Entirely," Dr. Grief replied. "I saw him as soon as the bandages came off. You have done extremely well."

"I was always the best. But that's what you paid

for." Baxter chuckled. His voice was oily. "And while we're on that subject, maybe we should talk about my final payment."

"You have already been paid the sum of one million dollars."

"Yes, Dr. Grief." Baxter smiled. "But I was wondering if you might not like to think about a little . . . bonus?"

"I thought we had an agreement." Dr. Grief turned his head very slowly. The red glasses homed in on the other man like searchlights.

"We had an agreement for my work, yes. But my silence is another matter. I was thinking of another quarter of a million. Given the size and the scope of your Gemini Project, it's not so much to ask. Then I'll retire to my little house in Spain and you'll never hear from me again."

"I will never hear from you again?"

"I promise."

Dr. Grief nodded. "Yes. I think that's a good idea."

His hand came out of his pocket. Alex saw that it was holding an automatic pistol with a thick silencer protruding from the barrel. Baxter was still smiling as Grief shot him once, through the middle of the forehead. He was thrown off his feet and onto the operating table. He lay still.

Dr. Grief lowered the gun. He went over to a telephone, picked it up, and dialed a number. There was a pause while his call was answered. Then . . .

"This is Grief. I have some garbage in the operating room that needs to be removed. Could you please inform the disposal team?"

He put down the phone and, glancing one last time at the still figure on the operating table, walked to the other side of the room. Alex saw him press a button. A section of the wall slid open to reveal an elevator on the other side. Dr. Grief got in. The doors closed.

Alex straightened up, too shocked to think straight. He staggered forward and went into the operating room. He knew he had to move fast. The disposal team that Dr. Grief had called for would be on their way. But he wanted to know what sort of operations took place here. Mr. Baxter had presumably been the surgeon. But for what sort of work had he been paid a million dollars?

Trying not to look at the body, Alex glanced around. On one shelf was a collection of surgical knives, as horrible as anything he had ever seen, the blades so sharp that he could almost feel their touch just by looking at them. There were rolls of gauze, syringes, and bottles containing various liquids. But nothing to say how Baxter had been employed. Alex realized it was hopeless. He knew nothing about medicine. This room could have been used for anything from ingrown toenails to full-blown heart surgery.

And then he saw the photographs. He recognized himself, lying on a bed that he thought he knew too. It was Paris! Room 13 at the Hotel du Monde. He remembered the black-and-white comforter, as well as the clothes he had been wearing that night. The clothes had been removed in most of the photographs. Every inch of him had been photographed, sometimes close up, sometimes wider. In every picture, his eyes were closed. Looking at himself, Alex knew that he had been drugged and, for the first time, remembered how the dinner with Mrs. Stellenbosch had ended.

The photographs disgusted him. He had been manipulated by people who thought he was worth nothing at all. From the moment he had met them, he had disliked Dr. Grief and his assistant director. Now he felt pure loathing. He still didn't know what they were doing. But they were evil. They had to be stopped.

He was shaken out of his thoughts by the sound

of footsteps coming up the stairs. The disposal team! He looked around him and cursed. He didn't have time to get out, and there was nowhere in the room to hide. Then he remembered the elevator. He went over to it and urgently stabbed at the button. The footsteps were getting nearer. He heard voices. Then the panels slid open. Alex stepped into a small, silver box. There were five buttons: *S, R, 1, 2,* and 3. He pressed *R.* He knew enough French to know that the *R* must stand for *Rez-de-chaussée* . . . or first floor. With luck, the elevator would take him back to where he had begun.

The doors slid shut a few seconds before the guards entered the operating room. Alex felt his stomach lurch as he was carried down. The elevator slowed. He realized that the doors could open anywhere. He might find himself surrounded by guards—or by the other boys in the school. Well, it was too late now. He had made his choice without thinking. He would just have to cope with whatever he found.

But he was lucky. The doors slid open to reveal the library. Alex assumed this was the real library and not another copy. The room was empty. He stepped out of the elevator, then turned around. He was facing the alcove. The elevator doors formed the alcove wall.

They were brilliantly camouflaged, with the suit of armor now sliced exactly in two, one half on each side. As the doors closed automatically, the armor slid back together again, completing the disguise. Despite himself, Alex had to admire the simplicity of it. The entire building was a fantastic box of tricks.

Alex looked at his hands. They were still filthy. He had almost forgotten that he was completely covered in soot. He crept out of the library, trying not to leave black footprints on the carpet. Then he hurried back to his room. When he got there, he had to remind himself that it was indeed his room and not the copy two floors above. But the CD player was there, and that was what he most needed.

He knew enough. It was time to call for the cavalry. He pressed the FAST FORWARD button three times, then went to take a shower.

12
DELAYING TACTICS

IT WAS RAINING IN LONDON, the sort of rain that seems never to stop. The early evening traffic was huddled together, going nowhere. Alan Blunt was standing at the window, looking out over the street, when there was a knock at the door. He turned away almost reluctantly, as if the city at its most damp and dismal held some attraction for him. Mrs. Jones came in. She was carrying a sheet of paper. As Blunt sat down behind his desk, he noticed the two words MOST URGENT printed in red across the top.

"We've heard from Alex," Mrs. Jones said.

"Oh, yes?"

"Smithers gave him a Euro-satellite transmitter built into a portable CD player. Alex sent a signal to us this morning, at eleven twenty-seven hours, his time."

"Meaning . . . ?"

"Either he's in trouble or he's found out enough for us to go in. Either way, we have to pull him out."

"I wonder . . ." Blunt leaned back in his chair, deep in thought. As a young man, he had gained a degree with honors in mathematics at Cambridge University. Thirty years later, he still saw life as only a series of complicated calculations. "Alex has been at Point Blanc for how long?" he asked.

"A week."

"As I recall, he didn't want to go. According to Sir David Friend, his behavior at Haverstock Hall was, to say the least, antisocial. Did you know that he knocked out Friend's daughter with a stun dart? Apparently, he also got her nearly killed in an incident in a railway tunnel."

Mrs. Jones sat down. "What are you saying, Alan?" she demanded.

"Only that Alex may not be one hundred percent reliable."

"He sent the message." Mrs. Jones couldn't keep the exasperation out of her voice. "For all we know, he could be in serious trouble. We gave him the device as an alarm signal, to let us know if he needed help. He's used it. We can't just sit back and do nothing."

"I wasn't suggesting that." Alan Blunt looked curiously at his head of operations. "You're not forming some sort of attachment to Alex Rider, are you?" he asked.

Mrs. Jones looked away. "Don't be ridiculous."

"You seem worried about him."

"He's fourteen years old, Alan! He's a child, for heaven's sake!"

"You used to have children."

"Yes." Mrs. Jones turned to face him again. "Perhaps that does make a difference. But even you must admit that he's special. We don't have another agent like him. A fourteen-year-old boy! The perfect secret weapon. My feelings about him have nothing to do with it. We can't afford to lose him."

"I just don't want to go blundering into Point Blanc without any firm information," Blunt said. "First of all, this is France we're talking about—and you know what the French are like. If we're seen to be invading their territory, they'll kick up one hell of a fuss. Secondly, Grief has got hold of boys from some of the wealthiest families in the world. If we go storming in with the SAS or whatever, the whole thing could blow up into a major international incident."

"You wanted proof that the school was connected

with the deaths of Roscoe and Ivanov," Mrs. Jones said. "Alex may have it."

"He may have it and he may not. A twenty-four-hour delay shouldn't make a great deal of difference."

"Twenty-four hours?"

"We'll put a unit on standby. They can keep an eye on things. If Alex is in trouble, we'll find out soon enough. It could play to our favor if he's managed to stir things up. It's exactly what we want. Force Grief to show his hand."

"And if Alex contacts us again?"

"Then we'll go in."

"We may be too late."

"For Alex?" Blunt showed no emotion. "I'm sure you don't need to worry about him, Mrs. Jones. He can look after himself."

The telephone rang, and Blunt answered it. The discussion was over. Mrs. Jones got up and left to make the arrangements for an SAS unit to fly into Geneva. Blunt was right, of course. Delaying tactics might work in their favor. Clear it with the French. Find out what was going on. And it was only twenty-four hours.

She would just have to hope Alex could survive that long.

Alex found himself eating his breakfast on his own. For the first time, James Sprintz had decided to join the other boys. There they were, the six of them, suddenly the best of friends. Alex looked carefully at the boy who had once been his friend, trying to see what it was that had changed about him. He knew the answer. It was everything and nothing. James was exactly the same and completely different at the same time.

He finished his food and got up. James called out to him. "Why don't you come to class this afternoon, Alex? It's Latin."

Alex shook his head. "Latin's a waste of time."

"Is that what you think?" James couldn't keep the sneer out of his voice, and for a moment Alex was startled. For just one second it hadn't been James talking at all. It had been James who had moved his mouth, but it had been Dr. Grief speaking the words.

"You enjoy it," Alex said. He hurried out of the room.

More than twenty hours had passed since he had pressed the FAST FORWARD button on the Discman. Alex wasn't sure what he had been expecting. A fleet of helicopters all flying the Union Jack would have been reassuring. But so far nothing had happened. He even wondered if the alarm signal had worked. At the same time, he was annoyed with himself. He had seen Grief shoot the man called Baxter in the operating room, and he had panicked. He knew that Grief was a killer. He knew that the academy was far more than the finishing school it pretended to be. But he still didn't have all the answers. What exactly was Dr. Grief doing? Had he been responsible for the deaths of Michael J. Roscoe and Viktor Ivanov—and if so, why?

The fact was, he didn't know enough. And by the time MI6 arrived, Dr. Baxter's body would be buried somewhere in the mountains and there would be nothing to suggest there was anything wrong. Alex would look like a fool. He could almost imagine Dr. Grief telling his side of the story . . .

"Yes. There is an operating room here. It was built years ago. We never use the top two floors. There is an elevator, yes. It was built before we came. We explained to Alex about the armed guards. They're here for his protection. But as you can see, gentlemen, there is nothing unpleasant happening here. The other boys are fine. Baxter? No, I don't know anyone by that name. Obviously Alex has been having bad dreams. I'm amazed that he was sent here to spy on us. I would ask you to take him with you when you leave. . . ."

He had to find out more—and that meant going back up to the third floor. Or perhaps down. Alex remembered the letters in the elevator. *R* for *Rez-de-chaussée.* *S* had to stand for *Sous-sol*—French for basement.

He went over to the Latin classroom and looked in through the half-open door. Dr. Grief was out of sight, but Alex could hear his voice.

"Felix qui potuit rerum cognoscere causus . . ."

There was the sound of scratching, chalk on a blackboard. And there were the six boys, sitting at their desks, listening intently. James was sitting between Hugo and Tom, taking notes. Alex looked at his watch. They would be there another hour. He was on his own.

He walked back down the corridor and slipped into the library. He had woken up still smelling faintly of soot and had no intention of making his way back up the chimney. Instead he crossed over to the suit of armor. He knew now that the alcove disguised a pair of elevator doors. They could be opened from inside. Presumably there was some sort of control on the outside too.

It took him just a few minutes to find it. There were three buttons built into the breastplate of the armor. Even up close, the buttons looked like part of the suit . . . something the medieval knight would have had to use to strap the thing on. But when Alex pressed the middle button, it moved. A moment later, the armor split in half again and he found himself looking into the waiting elevator.

This time he went down, not up. The elevator seemed to travel a long way, as if the basement of the building had been built far underground. Finally, the doors slid open again. Alex looked out onto a curving passageway with tiled walls that reminded him a little of a London subway station. The air was cold down here. The passage was lit by naked bulbs, screwed into the ceiling at intervals.

He looked out, then ducked back. A guard sat at a table at the end of the corridor, reading a newspaper. Would he have heard the elevator doors open? Alex leaned forward again. The guard was absorbed in the sports pages. He hadn't moved. Alex slipped out and crept down the passage, moving away from him. He reached the corner and turned into a second passageway lined with steel doors. There was nobody else in sight.

Where was he? There had to be something down here or there wouldn't be any need for a guard. Alex went over to the nearest door. There was a peephole set in the front, and he looked through into a bare, white cell with two bunk beds, a toilet, and a sink. There were two boys in the cell. One he had never seen before, but he recognized the other. It was the red-haired boy, Tom McMorin. But he had seen Tom in Latin class just a few minutes ago! What was he doing here?

Alex moved on to the next cell. This one also held two boys. One was a fair-haired, fit-looking boy with blue eyes and freckles. Once again, he recognized the other. It was James Sprintz. Alex examined the door. There were two bolts, but as far as he could see, no key. He drew back the bolts and jerked the door handle down. The door opened. He went in.

James stood up, astonished to see him. "Alex! What are you doing here?"

Alex closed the door. "We haven't got much time," he said. He was speaking in a whisper even though there was little chance of being overheard. "What happened to you?"

"They came for me the night before last," James

said. "They dragged me out of bed and into the library. There was some sort of elevator . . ."

"Behind the armor."

"Yes. I didn't know what they were doing. I thought they were going to kill me. But then they threw me in here."

"You've been here for two days?"

"Yes."

Alex shook his head. "I saw you having breakfast upstairs fifteen minutes ago."

"They've made duplicates of us." The other boy had spoken for the first time. He had an American accent. "All of us! I don't know how they've done it or why. But that's what they've done." He glanced at the door with anger in his eyes. "I've been here for months. My name's Paul Roscoe."

"Roscoe! Your dad's . . . ?"

"Michael Roscoe."

Alex fell silent. He couldn't tell this boy what had happened to his father and he looked away, afraid that Paul would read it in his eyes.

"How did you get down here?" James asked.

"Listen," Alex said. He was speaking rapidly now. "I was sent here by MI6. My name isn't Alex Friend.

It's Alex Rider. Everything's going to be okay. They'll send people in and get you all freed."

"You're a spy?" James was obviously startled.

Alex nodded. "I'm sort of a spy, I suppose," he said.

"You've opened the door. We can get out of here!" Paul Roscoe stood up, ready to move.

"No!" Alex held up his hands. "You've got to wait. There's no way down the mountain. Stay here for now and I'll come back with help. I promise you. It's the only way."

"I can't—"

"You have to. Trust me, Paul. I'm going to have to lock you back in so that nobody will know I've been here. But it won't be for long. I'll come back!"

Alex couldn't wait for any more argument. He went back to the door and opened it.

Mrs. Stellenbosch was standing outside.

He barely had time to register the shock of seeing her. He tried to bring up a hand to protect himself, to twist his body into position for a karate kick. But it was already too late. Her arm shot out, the heel of her hand driving into his face. It was like being hit by a brick wall. Alex felt every bone in his body rattle. White light exploded behind his eyes. Then he was out.

13

HOW TO RULE THE WORLD

"Open your eyes, Alex. Dr. Grief wishes to speak to you."

The words came from across an ocean. Alex groaned and tried to lift his head. He was sitting down, his arms pinned behind his back. The whole side of his face felt bruised and swollen, and the taste of blood was in his mouth. He opened his eyes and waited for the room to come into focus. Mrs. Stellenbosch was standing in front of him, her fist curled loosely in her other hand. Alex remembered the force of the blow that had knocked him out. His whole head was throbbing, and he ran his tongue over his teeth to see if any were missing. It was fortunate he had rolled with the punch. Otherwise she might have broken his neck.

Dr. Grief was sitting in his golden chair, watching Alex with what might have been curiosity or distaste or perhaps a little of both. There was nobody else in the room. It was still snowing outside, and a small fire burned in the hearth. The flames weren't as red as Dr. Grief's eyes.

"You have put us to a great deal of inconvenience," he said.

Alex straightened his head. He tried to move his hands, but they had been chained together behind the chair.

"Your name is not Alex Friend. You are not the son of Sir David Friend. Your name is Alex Rider, and you are employed by the British secret service." Dr. Grief was simply stating facts. There was no emotion in his voice.

"We have microphones concealed in the cells," Mrs. Stellenbosch explained. "Sometimes it is useful for us to hear the conversations between our young guests. Everything you said was overheard by the guard who summoned me."

"You have wasted our time and our money," Dr. Grief continued. "For that you will be punished. It is not a punishment you will survive."

The words were cold and absolute, and Alex felt the fear that they triggered. It coursed through his bloodstream, closing in on his heart. He took a deep breath, forcing himself back under control. He had signaled MI6. They would be on their way to Point Blanc. They might appear any minute now. He just had to play for time.

"You can't do anything to me," he said.

Mrs. Stellenbosch lashed out, and he was almost thrown backward as the back of her hand sliced into the side of his head. Only the chair kept him upright. "When you speak to the director, you will refer to him as 'Dr. Grief,' " she said.

Alex looked around again, his eyes watering. "You can't do anything to me, Dr. Grief," he said. "I know everything. I know about Project Gemini. And I've already told London what I know. If you do anything to me, they'll kill you. They're on their way here now."

Dr. Grief smiled, and in that single moment Alex knew that nothing he said would change what was about to happen to him. The man was too confident. He was like a poker player who had not only managed to see all the cards but had also stolen the four aces for himself.

"It may well be that your friends are on their way," he said. "But I do not think you have told them anything. We have been through your luggage and found the transmitting device concealed in the Discman. I note also that it is an ingenious electric saw. But as for the transmitter, it can send out a signal but not a message. How you learned about the Gemini Project is of no interest to me. I assume you overheard the name while eavesdropping at a door. We should have been more careful—but for British intelligence to send in a child . . . that was something we could not expect.

"Let us assume that your friends do come calling. They will find nothing wrong. You yourself will have disappeared. I shall tell them that you ran away. I will say that my men are looking for you even now, but that I very much fear you have died a cold and lingering death on the mountainside. Nobody will guess what I have done here. The Gemini Project will succeed. It has *already* succeeded. And even if your friends do take it upon themselves to kill me, it will make no difference. I cannot be killed, Alex. The world is already mine."

"You mean, it belongs to the kids you've hired to act as doubles," Alex said.

"Hired?" Dr. Grief muttered a few words to Mrs. Stellenbosch in a harsh, guttural language. Alex assumed it must be Afrikaans. Her thick lips parted and she laughed, showing heavy, discolored teeth. "Is that what you think?" Dr. Grief asked. "Is that what you believe?"

"I've seen them . . ."

"You don't know what you've seen. You have no understanding of my genius! Your little mind couldn't begin to encompass what I have achieved." Dr. Grief was breathing heavily. He seemed to come to a decision. "It is rare enough for me to come face-to-face with the enemy," he said. "It has always been my frustration that I will never be able to communicate to the world the brilliance of what I have done. Well, since I have you here—a captive audience, so to speak—I shall allow myself the luxury of describing the Gemini Project. And when you go, screaming, to your death, you will understand that there was never any hope for you. That you could not hope to come up against a man like me and win. Perhaps that will make it easier for you."

"I will smoke, if you don't mind, Doctor," Mrs. Stellenbosch said. She took out her cigars and lit one. Smoke danced in front of her eyes.

"I am, as I am sure you are aware, South African," Dr. Grief began. "The animals in the hall and in this room are all souvenirs of my time there, shot on safari. I still miss the country. It is the most beautiful place on this planet.

"What you may not know, however, is that for

many years I was one of South Africa's foremost bio-
chemists. I was head of the biology department at the
University of Johannesburg. I later ran the Cyclops In-
stitute for Genetic Research in Pretoria. But the height
of my career came in the 1960s when, although I was
still in my twenties, John Vorster, the president of
South Africa, appointed me minister of science."

"You've already said you're going to kill me," Alex
said, "but I didn't think that meant you were going
to bore me to death."

Mrs. Stellenbosch coughed on her cigar and ad-
vanced on Alex, her fist clenched. But Dr. Grief
stopped her. "Let the boy have his little joke," he said.
"There will be pain enough for him later."

The assistant director glowered at Alex, but returned to her seat. Dr. Grief went on. "I am telling
you this, Alex, only because it will help you understand. You perhaps know nothing about South Africa.
English schoolchildren are, I have found, the laziest
and most ignorant in the world. All that will soon
change! But let me tell you a little bit about my country, as it was when I was young.

"The white people of South Africa ruled everything. Under the laws that came to be known to the
world as apartheid, black people were not allowed to

live near white people. They could not marry white people. They could not share whites' toilets, restaurants, sports arenas, or bars. They had to carry passes. They were treated like animals."

"It was horrible," Alex said.

"It was wonderful!" Mrs. Stellenbosch murmured.

"It was indeed perfect," Dr. Grief agreed. "But as the years passed, I became aware that it would also be short-lived. The uprising at Soweto, the growing resistance, and the way the entire world—including your own stinking country—ganged up on us . . . I knew that white South Africa was doomed, and I even foresaw the day when power would be handed over to a man like Nelson Mandela."

"A criminal!" Mrs. Stellenbosch added. Smoke was dribbling out of her nostrils.

Alex said nothing. It was clear enough that both Dr. Grief and his assistant were mad. Just how mad they were was becoming clearer with every word they spoke.

"I looked at the world," Dr. Grief said, "and I began to see just how weak and pathetic it was becoming. How could it happen that a country like mine could be given away to people who had no idea how to run it? And why was the rest of the world so determined for it to be so? I looked around me and I saw that the people of America and Europe had become stupid and weak. The fall of the Berlin Wall only made things worse. I had always admired the Russians, but they quickly became infected with the same disease. And I thought to myself, If I ruled the world, how much stronger it would be. How much better . . ."

"For you, perhaps, Dr. Grief," Alex said. "But not for anyone else."

Grief ignored him. His eyes, behind the red glasses, were brilliant. "It has been the dream of very few men to rule the entire world," he said. "Hitler was one. Napoleon another. Stalin, perhaps, a third. Great men! Remarkable men! But to rule the world in the twenty-first century requires something more than military strength. The world is a more complicated place now. Where does real power lie? Oh, yes—in politics. Prime ministers and presidents. But you will also find power in industry, in science, in the media, in oil, in the Internet. . . . Modern life is a great tapestry, and if you wish to take control of it all, you must seize hold of every strand.

"This is what I decided to do, Alex. And it was because of my unique position in the unique place that was South Africa that I was able to attempt it." Grief took a deep breath. "What do you know about nuclear transplantation?" he asked.

"I don't know anything," Alex said. "But as you said, I'm an English schoolboy. Lazy and ignorant."

"There is another word for it. Have you heard of cloning?"

Alex almost burst out laughing. "You mean, like Dolly the sheep?"

"To you it may be a joke, Alex. Something out of science fiction. But scientists have been searching for a way to create replicas of themselves for more than a hundred years. The word itself is Greek."

"The Greek word for twig," Mrs. Stellenbosch muttered.

"Think how a twig starts as one branch but then splits into two," Grief continued. "This is exactly what has been achieved with lizards, with sea urchins, with tadpoles and frogs, with mice and—yes—on the fifth of July, 1996, with a sheep. The theory is simple enough. Nuclear transplantation: to take the nucleus out of an egg and to replace it with a cell taken from an adult. I won't tire you with the details, Alex. But it is not a joke. Dolly was the perfect copy of a sheep that had died six years earlier. She was the result of no less than one hundred years of experimentation.

And in all that time, the scientists shared a single dream: to clone an adult human. Well . . . I have achieved that dream!"

He paused.

"If you want a round of applause, you'll have to take off the handcuffs," Alex said.

"I don't want applause," Grief snarled. "Not from you. What I want from you is your life, and that I will take."

"So who did you clone?" Alex asked. "Not Mrs. Stellenbosch, I hope. I'd have thought one of her was more than enough."

"Who do you think? I cloned myself!" Dr. Grief grabbed hold of the arms of his chair, a king on a throne of his own imagination. "Twenty years ago I began my work," he explained. "I told you—I was minister of science. I had all the equipment and money I needed. Also, this was South Africa! The rules that hampered other scientists around the world did not apply to me. I was able to use human beings— political prisoners—for my experiments. Everything was done in secret. I worked without stopping for twenty years. And then, when I was ready, I stole a very large amount of money from the South African government and moved here.

"This was in 1981. And six years later, almost a whole decade before an English scientist astonished the world by cloning a sheep, I did something far, far more extraordinary . . . here, at Point Blanc. I cloned myself. Not just once! Sixteen times. Sixteen exact copies of me. With my looks. My brains. My ambition. And my determination."

"Were they all as mad as you too?" Alex asked, and he flinched as Mrs. Stellenbosch hit him again, this time in the stomach. But he wanted to make them angry. If they were angry, they might make mistakes.

"To begin with, they were babies," Dr. Grief said. "Sixteen babies who would grow up to become replicas of myself. I have had to wait fourteen years for the babies to become boys and the boys to become teenagers. Eva here has been a mother to all of them. You have met them . . . some of them."

"Tom, Cassian, Nicolas, Hugo, Joe. And James . . ." Now Alex understood why they had somehow all looked the same.

"Do you see, Alex? Do you have any idea what I have done? I will never die because even when this body is finished with, I will live on in them. I *am* them and they are me. We are one and the same."

He smiled again. "I was helped in all this by Eva,

who had also worked with me in the South African government. She had worked in BOSS—our own secret service. She was one of their principal interrogators."

"Happy days!" Mrs. Stellenbosch muttered.

"Together we set up the academy. Because, you see, that was the second part of my plan. I had created sixteen copies of myself. But that wasn't enough. You remember what I said about the strands of the tapestry? I had to bring them here, to draw them together."

"To replace them with copies of yourself!" Suddenly Alex saw it all. It was totally insane. But it was the only way to make sense of everything he had seen.

Dr. Grief nodded. "It was my observation that families with wealth and power frequently had children who were troubled. Parents with no time for their sons. Sons with no love for their parents. These children became my targets, Alex. Because, you see, I wanted what these children had.

"Take a boy like Hugo Vries. One day his father will leave him with a fifty percent stake in the world's diamond market. Or Tom McMorin. His mother has newspapers all over the world. Or Joe Canterbury. His father at the Pentagon, his mother a senator. What better start for a life in politics? What better start for a future president of the United States, even? Fifteen of the most promising children who have been sent here to Point Blanc, I have replaced with copies of myself. Surgically altered, of course, to look exactly like the original thing."

"Baxter . . . the man you shot . . ."

"You have been busy, Alex." For the first time, Dr. Grief looked surprised. "The late Mr. Baxter was a plastic surgeon. I found him working in Harley Street, in London. He had gambling debts. It was easy to bring him under my control, and it was his job to operate on my family, to change their faces, their skin color, and where necessary their bodies so that they would exactly resemble the teenagers they replaced. From the moment the real teenagers arrived here at Point Blanc, they were kept under observation."

"With identical rooms on the third and fourth floors."

"Yes. My doubles were able to watch their targets on television monitors. To copy their every movement. To learn their mannerisms. To eat like them. To speak like them. In short, to become them."

"It would never have worked!" Alex twisted in his chair, trying to find some leverage in the handcuffs.

But the metal was too tight. He couldn't move. "Parents would know that the children you sent back were fakes!" he insisted. "Any mother would know it wasn't her son, even if he looked the same."

Mrs. Stellenbosch giggled. She had finished her cigar. Now she lit another.

"You're quite wrong, Alex," Dr. Grief said. "In the first place, you are talking about busy, hardworking parents who had little or no time for their children in the first place. And you forget that the very reason these people sent their sons here was because they *wanted* them to change. It is the reason all parents send their sons to private schools. Oh, yes, they think the schools will make their children better, more clever, more confident. They would actually be disappointed if those children came back the same.

"And nature, too, is on our side. A boy of fourteen leaves home for six or seven months. By the time he gets back, nature will have made its mark. The boy will be taller. He will be fatter or thinner. Even his voice will have changed. It's all part of puberty, and the parents when they see him will say, 'Oh, Tom, you've gotten so big, and you're so grown-up!' And they will suspect nothing. In fact, they would be worried if the boy *hadn't* changed."

"But Roscoe guessed, didn't he?" Alex knew that he had arrived at the truth, the reason he had been sent here in the first place. He knew why Roscoe and Ivanov had died.

"There have been two occasions when the parents did not believe what they saw," Dr. Grief admitted. "Michael J. Roscoe in New York. And General Major Viktor Ivanov in Moscow. Neither man completely guessed what had happened. But they were unhappy. They argued with their sons. They asked too many questions."

"And the sons told you what had happened."

"You might say that I told myself. The sons, after all, are me. But yes. Michael Roscoe knew something was wrong and called MI6 in London. I presume that is how you were unlucky enough to be involved. I had to pay to have Roscoe killed just as I paid for the death of Ivanov. But it was to be expected that there would be problems. Two out of sixteen is not so catastrophic, and of course it makes no difference to my plans. In many ways, it even helps me. Michael J. Roscoe left his entire fortune to his son. And I understand that the Russian president is taking a personal interest in Dimitry Ivanov, following the loss of his father.

"In short, the Gemini Project has been an

outstanding success. In a few days' time, the last of the children will leave Point Blanc to take their places in the heart of their family. Once I am satisfied that they have all been accepted, I will, I fear, have to dispose of the originals. They will die painlessly.

"The same cannot be said for you, Alex Rider. You have caused me a great deal of annoyance. I propose, therefore, to make an example of you." Dr. Grief reached into his pocket and took out a device that looked like a pager. It contained a single button, which he pressed. "What is the first lesson tomorrow morning, Eva?" he asked.

"Biology," Mrs. Stellenbosch replied.

"As I thought. You have perhaps been to biology classes where a frog or a rat has been dissected, Alex?" he asked. "For some time now, my children have been asking to see a human dissection. This is no surprise to me. I myself first attended a human dissection at the age of fourteen. Tomorrow morning, at half past nine, their wish will be granted. You will be brought into the laboratory and we shall open you up and have a look at you. We will not use anesthetic, and it will be interesting to see how long you survive before your heart gives out. And then, of course, we shall dissect your heart."

"You're sick!" Alex yelled. Now he was thrashing about in the chair, trying to break the wood, trying to get the handcuffs to come apart. But it was hopeless. The metal cut into him. The chair rocked but stayed in one piece. "You're a madman!"

"I am a scientist!" Dr. Grief spat the words. "And that is why I am giving you a scientific death. At least in your last minutes you will have been of some use to me." He looked past Alex. "Take him away and search him thoroughly. Then lock him up for the night. I'll see him again first thing tomorrow morning."

Alex had seen Dr. Grief summon the guards, but he hadn't heard them come in. He was seized from behind, the handcuffs were unlocked, and he was jerked backward out of the room. His last sight of Dr. Grief was of the man stretching out his hands to warm them in the fire, the twisting flames reflected in his glasses. Mrs. Stellenbosch smiled and blew out smoke.

Then the door slammed shut and Alex was dragged down the corridor knowing that Blunt and the secret service had to be on their way, but wondering whether they would arrive before it was too late.

14

BLACK RUN

THE CELL MEASURED SIX feet by twelve and contained a bunk bed with no mattress and a chair. Moonlight slanted in through a small, heavily barred window high up on the wall. The door was solid steel. Alex had heard a key turn in the lock after it was closed. He had not been given anything to eat or drink. The cell was cold, but there were no blankets on the bed.

At least the guards had left the handcuffs off. They had searched Alex expertly, removing everything they had found in his pockets. They had also removed his belt and the laces of his shoes. Perhaps Dr. Grief had thought he would hang himself. He needed Alex fresh and alive for the biology lesson.

It was about two o'clock in the morning, but Alex hadn't slept. He had tried to put out of his mind everything Grief had told him. That wasn't important now. He knew that he had to escape before 9:30

because—like it or not—it seemed he was on his own. More than thirty-six hours had passed since he had pressed the panic button that Smithers had given him, and nothing had happened. Either the machine hadn't worked or for some reason MI6 had decided not to come. Of course, it was possible that something might happen before breakfast the next day. But Alex wasn't prepared to risk it. He had to get out. Tonight.

For the twentieth time he went over to the door and knelt down, listening carefully. The guards had dragged him back down to the basement. He was in a corridor separate from the other prisoners. Although everything had happened very quickly, Alex had tried to remember where he had been taken. Out of the elevator and to the left. Around the corner and then down a second passageway to a door at the end. He was on his own. And listening through the door, he was fairly sure that they hadn't posted a guard outside.

Alex had one bit of hope to cling to. When the guards had searched him, they hadn't quite taken everything. Neither of them had even noticed the golden stud in his ear. What had Smithers said?

"It's a small but very powerful explosive device, like a miniature grenade. Separating the two pieces

activates it. Count to ten and it'll blow a hole in just about anything."

Now was the time to put it to the test.

Alex reached up and unscrewed the ear stud. He pulled it out of his ear, slipped the two pieces into the keyhole of the door, stepped back, and counted to ten.

Nothing happened. Was the stud broken, like the Discman transmitter? Alex was about to give up when there was a sudden flash, an intense sheet of orange flame. Fortunately there was no noise. The flare continued for about five seconds, then went out. Alex went back to the door. The stud had burned a hole in it, the size of a silver dollar. The melted metal was still glowing. Alex reached out and pushed. The door swung open.

Alex felt a momentary surge of excitement, but he forced himself to remain calm. He might be out of the cell, but he was still in the basement of the academy. There were guards everywhere. He was on top of a mountain with no skis and no obvious way down. He wasn't safe yet. Not by a long way.

He slipped out of the room and followed the corridor back around to the elevator. He was tempted to find the other boys and release them, but he knew they couldn't help. Taking them out of their cells would only put them in danger. Somehow, he found his way back to the elevator. He noticed that the guard post he had seen that morning was empty. Either the man had gone to make himself coffee or Grief had relaxed security in the academy. With Alex and all the other boys locked up, there was nobody left to guard. Or so they thought. Alex hurried forward.

He took the elevator back to the second floor. He knew that his only way off the mountain lay in his bedroom. Grief would certainly have examined everything he had brought with him. But what would he have done with it? Alex crept down the dimly lit corridor and into the room. And there it all was, lying in a heap on his bed. The ski suit. The goggles. Even the Discman with the Beethoven CD. Alex heaved a sigh of relief. He was going to need all of it.

He had already worked out what he was going to do. He couldn't ski off the mountain because he still had no idea where the skis were kept. But there was more than one way to take to the snow. Alex froze as a guard walked along the corridor outside the room. So not everyone at the academy was asleep! He would have to move fast. As soon as the broken cell door was discovered, the alarm would be raised.

He waited until the guard had gone, then stole into

the laundry room a few doors down. When he came out, he was carrying a long, flat object made of light-weight aluminum. He carried it into his bedroom, closed the door, and turned on one small lamp. He was afraid the guard would see the light if he returned. But he couldn't work in the dark. It was a risk he had to take.

He had stolen an ironing board.

Alex had been snowboarding only three times in his life. The first time, he had spent most of the day falling or sitting on his bottom. Snowboarding is a lot harder to learn than skiing, but as soon as you get the hang of it, you can advance fast. By the third day, Alex had learned how to ride, edging and cutting his way down the beginner slopes. He needed a snowboard now. The ironing board would have to do.

He picked up the Discman and turned it on. The Beethoven CD spun, then slid forward, its diamond edge jutting out. Alex made a mental calculation, then began to cut. The ironing board was wider than he would have liked. He knew that the longer the board, the faster he could go, but if he left it too long, he would have no control. The ironing board was flat. Without any curve at the front—or the nose, as it was called—he would be at the mercy of every bump or upturned root. He pressed down. The spinning disc sliced through the metal. Carefully, Alex drew it around, forming a curve. One end of the ironing board fell away. He picked up the other. It came up to his chest. Perfect.

Now he sliced off the supports, leaving about six inches sticking up. He knew that the rider and the board can work together only if the bindings are right, and he had nothing . . . no boots, no straps, and no highback to support his heel. He was just going to have to improvise. He tore two strips of sheet from the bed, then slipped into his ski suit. He would have to tie one of his sneakers to what was left of the ironing board supports. It was horribly dangerous. If he fell, he would dislocate his foot.

But he was almost ready. Quickly, Alex zipped up the ski suit. Smithers had said it was bulletproof, and it occurred to him that he was probably going to need it. He put the goggles around his neck. The window still hadn't been repaired. He dropped the ironing board out, then climbed out after it.

There was no moon. Alex found the switch concealed in the goggles and turned it. He heard a soft hum as the concealed battery activated. Suddenly the side of the mountain glowed an eerie green and Alex was able to see the trees, the deserted ski run, and the side of the mountain, falling away.

Carefully, he took up his position on the ironing board, his right foot at forty degrees, his left foot at twenty. He was goofy-footed. That was what the instructor had told him. His feet should have been the other way around. But this was no time to worry about technique. Instead, he used the strips of torn sheet to tie the ironing board to his feet, then he stood where he was, contemplating what he was about to do. He had only traveled down green and blue runs—the colors given to the beginners' and intermediate slopes. He knew from James that this mountain was an expert black all the way down. His breath rose up in green clouds in front of his eyes. Could he do it? Could he trust himself?

An alarm bell exploded behind him. Lights came on throughout the academy. Alex pushed forward and set off, picking up speed with every second. The decision had been made for him. Now, whatever happened, there could be no going back.

Dr. Grief, wearing a long silver dressing gown, stood beside the open window in Alex's room. Mrs. Stellenbosch was also wearing a dressing gown. Hers was pink silk and looked strangely hideous, hanging off her lumpy body. Three guards stood watching them, waiting for instructions.

"Who searched the boy?" Dr. Grief asked. He had already been shown the cell door with the circular hole burned into the lock.

None of the guards answered, but their faces had gone pale.

"This is a question to be answered in the morning," Dr. Grief continued. "For now, all that matters is that we find him and kill him."

"He must be walking down the mountainside," Mrs. Stellenbosch said. "He has no skis. He won't make it. We can wait until morning and pick him up in the helicopter."

"I think the boy may be more inventive than we believe." Dr. Grief picked up the remains of the ironing board. "You see? He has improvised some sort of sleigh or toboggan. All right . . ." He had come to a decision. Mrs. Stellenbosch was glad to see the certainty return to his eyes. "I want two men on snowmobiles, following him down. Now!" One of the guards hurried out of the room.

"What about the unit at the foot of the mountain?" Mrs. Stellenbosch said.

"Indeed." Dr. Grief smiled. He had always kept a man and a driver at the end of the last valley in case anybody ever tried to leave the academy on skis. It was a precaution that was about to pay off. "Alex Rider will have to arrive in La Vallée de Fer. Whatever he's using to get down, he'll be unable to cross the railway line. We can have a machine gun set up, waiting for him. Assuming he does manage to get that far, he'll be a sitting duck."

"Excellent," Mrs. Stellenbosch purred.

"I would have liked to watch him die. But, yes. The Rider boy has no hope at all. And we can return to bed."

Alex was on the edge of space, seemingly falling to his certain death. In snowboarding language, he was catching air, meaning that he had shot away from the ground. With every foot he went forward, the mountainside disappeared another five feet downward. He felt the world spin around him. Wind whipped into his face. Then somehow he had brought himself in line with the next section of the slope and shot down, steering the ironing board ever farther from Point Blanc. He was moving at a terrifying speed, trees and rock formations passing in a luminous green blur across his night-vision goggles. In some ways, the steeper slopes made it easier. Once, he had tried to make a landing on a flat part of the mountain—a tabletop—to slow himself down. He had hit the ground with such a bone-shattering crash that he had almost blacked out and had taken the next twenty yards almost totally blind.

The ironing board was shuddering and shaking crazily, and it took all his strength to make the turns. He was trying to follow the natural fall line of the mountain, but there were too many obstacles in the way. What he most dreaded was melted snow. If the board landed on a patch of mud at this speed, he would be thrown and killed. And he knew that the farther down he went, the greater the danger would become.

But he had been traveling for several minutes and so far he had fallen only twice—both times into thick banks of snow that had protected him. How far down could it be? He tried to remember what James Sprintz had told him, but thinking was impossible at this speed. He was having to use every ounce of his conscious thought simply to stay upright.

He reached a small lip where the surface was level and drove the edge of the board into the snow, bringing himself to a skidding halt. Ahead of him, the ground fell away again alarmingly. He hardly dared look down. There were thick clumps of trees to the left and to the right. In the distance there was just a green blur. The goggles could see only so far.

And then he heard the sound coming up behind him. The scream of at least two—maybe more—engines. Alex looked back over his shoulder. For a moment there was nothing. But then he saw them, black flies swimming into his field of vision. There were two of them, heading his way.

Grief's men were riding specially adapted Yamaha Mountain Max snowmobiles equipped with 700 cc triple-cylinder engines. The bikes were flying over the ice on their 141-inch tracks, effortlessly moving five times faster than Alex. The 300-watt headlights had already picked him up. Now the men sped toward him, halving the distance between them with almost every second that passed.

Alex leapt forward, diving into the next slope. At the same time, there was a sudden chatter, a series of distant cracks, and the snow flew up all around him. Grief's men had machine guns built into their snowmobiles! Alex yelled as he swooped down the mountainside, barely able to control the sheet of metal under his feet. The makeshift binding was tearing at his ankles. The whole thing was vibrating crazily. He couldn't see. He could only hang on, trying to keep his balance, hoping that the way ahead was clear.

The headlights of the nearest Yamaha shot out, and Alex saw his own shadow, stretching ahead of him on the snow. There was another chatter from the machine gun and Alex ducked, almost feeling the fan of bullets spray over his head. The second bike screamed up, coming parallel with him. He had to get off the mountainside. Otherwise he would be shot or run over. Or both.

He forced the board onto its edge, making a turn. He had seen a gap in the trees and he made for it. Now he was racing through the forest, with branches and trunks whipping past like crazy animations in a computer game. Could the snowmobiles follow him through here? The question was answered by another burst from the machine gun, ripping through the leaves and branches. Alex searched for a narrower path. The board shuddered, and he was almost thrown headfirst. The snow was getting thinner! He edged and turned, heading for two of the thickest trees. He passed between them with inches to spare.

The Yamaha snowmobile had no choice. The rider

had run out of paths, and was traveling too fast to stop. He tried to follow Alex between the trees, but the snowmobile was too wide. Alex heard the collision. There was a terrible crunch, then a scream, then an explosion. A ball of orange flame leapt over the trees, sending the black shadows in a crazy dance. Ahead of him, Alex saw another hillock and beyond it, a gap in the trees. It was time to leave the forest.

He swooped up the hillock and out, once again catching air. As he left the trees behind him, six feet in the air, he saw the second snowmobile. It had caught up with him. For a moment, the two of them were side by side. Alex doubled forward and grabbed the nose of his board. Still in midair, he twisted the tip of the board, bringing the tail swinging around. He had timed it perfectly. The tail slammed into the second rider's head, almost throwing him out of his seat. Alex fought for balance. The rider yelled and lost control. His snowmobile jerked sideways as if trying to make an impossibly tight turn. Then it left the ground, cartwheeling over and over. The rider was thrown off, then screamed as the snowmobile completed its final turn and landed on top of him. Man and machine bounced across the surface of the snow and lay still. Meanwhile, Alex had slammed into the snow and skidded to a halt, his breath clouding, green, in front of his eyes.

A minute later, he pushed off again. Ahead of him, he could see that all the trails were leading into a single valley. This must be the bottleneck called La Vallée de Fer. He'd actually done it! He'd reached the bottom of the mountain. But now he was trapped. There was no other way around. He could see lights in the distance. A city. Safety. But he could also see the railway line stretching right across the valley, from the left to the right, protected on both sides by an embankment and a barbed-wire fence. The glow from the city illuminated everything. On one side the track came out of the mouth of a tunnel. It ran for about a hundred yards in a straight line before a sharp bend carried it around the other side of the valley and it disappeared from sight.

The two men in the gray van saw Alex snowboarding toward them. They were parked on a road on the other side of the railway line and had been waiting only a few minutes. They hadn't seen the explosion and wondered what had happened to the two men on their snowmobiles. But that wasn't their concern. Their orders were to kill the boy. And there he was, right out in the open, expertly managing the last slope down through the valley. Every second brought him closer to them. There was nowhere for him to hide. The machine gun was a Belgian FN MAG and would cut him in half.

Alex saw the van. He saw the machine gun aimed at him. He couldn't stop. It was too late to change direction. He had come this far, but now he was finished. He felt the strength draining out of him. Where was MI6? Why did he have to die, out here, on his own?

And then there was a sudden blast as a train exploded out of the tunnel. It was a freight train, traveling about twenty miles an hour. It had at least thirty train cars being pulled by a diesel engine, and it formed a moving wall between Alex and the gun, protecting him. But it would be there only a few seconds. He had to move fast.

Barely knowing what he was doing, Alex found a last mound of snow and, using it as a launch pad, swept up into the air. Now he was level with the train . . . now above it. He shifted his weight and came down onto the roof of one of the cars. The surface was covered in ice, and for a moment he thought he would fall off the other side, but he managed to swing around so that he was snowboarding along the roofs of the cars, jumping from one to another while being swept along the track—away from the gun—in a blast of freezing air.

He had done it! He had gotten away! He was still sliding forward, the train adding its speed to his own. No snowboarder had ever moved so fast. But then the train reached the bend in the track. The board had nothing to keep it from sliding on the icy surface. As the train sped around to the left, centrifugal force threw Alex to the right. Once again he soared into the air. But he had finally run out of snow.

Alex hit the ground like a rag doll. The snowboard was torn off his feet. He bounced twice, then hit a wire fence and came to rest with blood spreading around a deep gash in his head. His eyes were closed.

The train plowed on through the night. Alex lay still.

15

AFTER THE FUNERAL

THE GREEN-AND-WHITE ambulance raced down
the Avenue Maquis de Gresivaudan in the north of
Grenoble, heading toward the river. It was five o'clock
in the morning and there was no traffic yet, no need
for the siren. Just before the river it turned off into a
compound of ugly, modern buildings. This was the
second-biggest hospital in the city. The ambulance
pulled up outside SERVICE DES URGENCES—the emer-
gency room. Paramedics ran toward it as the back
doors flew open.

Mrs. Jones got out of her taxi and watched as the
limp, unmoving body of a boy was lowered on a
stretcher, transferred to a gurney, and rushed in
through the double doors. There was already a saline
drip attached to his arm, and an oxygen mask covered
his face. It had been snowing up in the mountains, but
down here there was only a dull drizzle sweeping
across the pavements. A doctor in a white coat was

bending over the stretcher. He sighed and shook his head. Mrs. Jones had seen this. She crossed the road and followed the stretcher in.

A thin man with close-cropped hair wearing a black sweater and vest had also been watching the hospital. He saw Mrs. Jones without knowing who she was. He had also seen Alex. He took out a cell phone and made a call. Dr. Grief would want to know. . . .

Three hours later, the sun had risen over the city. Grenoble is largely modern, and even with its perfect mountain setting, it still struggles to be attractive. On this damp, cloudy day it was clearly failing. Outside the hospital, another car drew up and Eva Stellenbosch got out. She was wearing a silver-and-white-checked suit with a hat perched on her ginger hair. She carried a leather handbag, and for once she had put on makeup. She wanted to look elegant. She looked like a man in drag.

She walked into the hospital and found the main reception desk. A young nurse sat behind a bank of telephones and computer screens. Mrs. Stellenbosch addressed her in fluent French.

"Excuse me," she said. "I understand that a young boy was brought here this morning. His name is Alex Friend."

"One moment, please." The nurse entered the name in her computer. She read the information on the screen and her face became serious. "May I ask who you are?"

"I am the assistant director of the Academy at Point Blanc. He is one of our students."

"Are you aware of the extent of his injuries, madame?"

"I was told that he was involved in a snowboard accident." Mrs. Stellenbosch took out a small hand-kerchief and dabbed at her eye.

"He tried to snowboard down the mountain at night. He was involved in a collision with a train. His injuries are very serious, madame. The doctors are operating on him now."

Mrs. Stellenbosch nodded, swallowing her tears. "My name is Eva Stellenbosch," she said. "May I wait for any news?"

"Of course, madame."

Mrs. Stellenbosch took a seat in the reception area. For the next hour, she watched as people came and went, some walking, some in wheelchairs. There were other people waiting for news of other patients. One of them, she noticed, was a serious-looking woman with badly cut black hair and very black eyes.

She was no doubt from England, as she was periodically glancing at a copy of the *London Times*.

Then a door opened and a doctor in a white coat came out. Doctors have a certain face when they come to give bad news. This doctor had it now. "Madame Stellenbosch?" he asked.

"Yes?"

"You are the director of the school?"

"The assistant director. Yes."

The doctor sat next to her. "I am very sorry, madame. Alex Friend died a few minutes ago." He waited while she absorbed the news. "He had multiple fractures: his arms, his collarbone, his leg. He had also fractured his skull. We operated, but unfortunately there had been massive internal bleeding. He went into shock and we were unable to bring him around."

Mrs. Stellenbosch nodded, struggling for words. "I must notify his family," she whispered.

"Is he from this country?"

"No. He is English. His father . . . Sir David Friend . . . I'll have to tell him." Mrs. Stellenbosch got to her feet. "Thank you, Doctor. I'm sure you did everything you could."

Out of the corner of her eye, Mrs. Stellenbosch

noticed that the woman with the black hair had also stood up, letting her newspaper fall to the floor. She had overheard the conversation. She looked shocked.

Both women left the hospital at the same time. Neither of them spoke.

The aircraft waiting on the runway was a Lockheed Martin C-130 Hercules. It had landed just after midday. Now it waited beneath the clouds while three vehicles drove toward it. One was a police car, one a Jeep, and one an ambulance.

The Saint-Geoirs airport at Grenoble does not see many international flights, but the plane had flown out that morning from England. From the other side of the perimeter fence, Mrs. Stellenbosch watched through a pair of high-powered binoculars. A small military escort had been formed. Four men in French uniforms had lifted up a coffin that seemed pathetically small when balanced on their broad shoulders. The coffin was simple: pine wood with silver handles. A Union Jack was folded into a square in the middle.

Marching in time, they carried the coffin toward the waiting plane. Mrs. Stellenbosch focused the binoculars and saw the woman from the hospital. She had been traveling in the police car. She stood watching as the coffin was loaded into the plane, then got back into the car and was driven away. By now, Mrs. Stellenbosch knew who she was. Dr. Grief kept extensive files and had quickly identified her as Mrs. Jones, head of Special Operations for MI6 and number two to its chief, Alan Blunt.

Mrs. Stellenbosch stayed until the end. The doors of the plane were closed. The Jeep and the ambulance left. The plane's propellers began to turn, and it lumbered forward onto the runway. A few minutes later it took off. As it thundered into the air, the clouds opened as if to receive it, and for a moment its silver wings were bathed in brilliant sunlight. Then the clouds rolled back and the plane disappeared.

Mrs. Stellenbosch dialed a number on her cell phone and waited until she was connected. "The little swine has gone," she said.

She got back into her car and drove away.

After Mrs. Jones left the airport, she returned to the hospital and took the stairs to the second floor. She came to a pair of doors guarded by a policeman, who nodded and let her pass through. On the other side

was a corridor leading to a private wing. She walked
down to a door, this one also guarded by a policeman.
She didn't knock, but went straight in.

Alex Rider was standing by the window, looking
out at the view of Grenoble on the other side of the
River Isére. High above him, five steel and glass bubbles moved slowly along a cable, ferrying tourists up
to the Fort de la Bastille. He turned around as Mrs.
Jones came in. There was a bandage around his head,
but otherwise he seemed unhurt.

"You're lucky to be alive," she said.

"I thought I was dead," Alex replied.

"Let's hope that Dr. Grief believes as much." Despite herself, Mrs. Jones couldn't keep the worry out
of her eyes. "It really was a miracle," she said. "You
should have at least broken something."

"The ski suit protected me," Alex said. He tried to
think back to the whirling, desperate moment when
he had been thrown off the train. "There was under-
growth. And the fence sort of caught me." He rubbed
his leg and winced. "Even if it was barbed wire."

He walked back to the bed and sat down. After
they had finished examining him, the French doctors
had brought him fresh clothes. Military clothes, he no-

ticed. Combat jacket and trousers. He hoped they weren't trying to tell him something.

"I've got three questions," he said. "But let's start with the big one. I called for help two days ago. Where were you?"

"I'm very sorry, Alex," Mrs. Jones said. "There were . . . logistical problems."

"Yes? Well, while you were having your logistical problems, Dr. Grief was getting ready to cut me up!"

"We couldn't just storm the academy. That could have gotten you killed. It could have gotten you all killed. We had to move in slowly—try to work out what was going on. How do you think we found you so quickly?"

"That was my second question."

Mrs. Jones shrugged. "We've had people in the mountains ever since we got your signal. They've been closing in on the academy. They heard the machine-gun fire when the snowmobiles were chasing you and followed you down on skis. They saw what happened with the train and radioed for help."

"All right. So why all the business with the funeral? Why do you want Dr. Grief to think I'm dead?"

"That's simple, Alex. From what you've told us,

he's keeping fifteen boys prisoner in the academy. These are the boys that he plans to replace." She shook her head. "I have to say, it's the most incredible thing I've ever heard. And I wouldn't have believed it if I'd heard it from anyone else except you."

"You're too kind," Alex muttered.

"If Dr. Grief thought you'd survived last night, the first thing he would do is kill every one of those boys. Or perhaps he'd use them as hostages. We had only one hope if we were going to take him by surprise. He had to believe you were dead."

"You're going to take him by surprise?"

"We're going in tonight. I told you. We've assembled an attack squad here in Grenoble. They were up in the mountains last night. They plan to set off as soon as it's dark. They're armed and they're experienced." Mrs. Jones hesitated. "There's just one thing they don't have."

"And what's that?" Alex asked, feeling a sudden sense of unease.

"They need someone who knows the building," Mrs. Jones said. "The library, the secret elevator, the placement of the guards, the passage with the cells . . ."

"Oh, no!" Alex exclaimed. Now he understood the military clothes. "Forget it! I'm not going back up there. I almost got killed trying to get away! Do you think I'm crazy?"

"Alex, you'll be looked after. You'll be completely safe."

"No!"

Mrs. Jones nodded. "All right. I can understand your feelings. But there's someone I want you to meet."

As if on cue, there was a knock on the door. It opened to reveal a young man, also in combat dress. The man was well built with black hair, square shoulders, and a dark, watchful face. He was in his late twenties. He saw Alex and shook his head. "Well, well, well. There's a surprise," he said. "How's it going, Cub?"

Alex recognized him at once. It was the soldier he had known as Wolf. When MI6 had sent him for eleven days' SAS training in Wales, Wolf had been in charge of his unit. If training had been hell, Wolf had only made it worse, picking on Alex from the start and almost getting him thrown out. In the end, though, it had been Wolf who had nearly lost his place with the SAS, and Alex who had saved him. But Alex still wasn't sure where that left him, and the other man was giving nothing away.

"Wolf!" Alex said.

"I heard you got busted up." Wolf shrugged. "I'm sorry. I forgot the flowers and the fruit basket."

"What are you doing here?" Alex asked.

"They called me in to clear up the mess you left behind."

"So where were you when I was being chased down the mountain?"

"It seems you were doing fine on your own."

Mrs. Jones took over. "Alex has done a very good job up to now," she said. "But the fact is that there are fifteen young prisoners up at Point Blanc and our first priority must be to save them. From what Alex has told us, we know there are about thirty guards in and around the school. The only chance those boys have is for an SAS unit to break in. It's happening tonight." She turned to Alex. "The unit will be commanded by Wolf."

The SAS never uses rank when it is on active service. Mrs. Jones was careful only to use Wolf's code name.

"Where does the boy come into this?" Wolf demanded.

"He knows the school. He knows the position of

the guards and the location of the prison cells. He can lead you to the elevator."

"He can tell us everything we need to know here and now," Wolf interrupted. He turned to Mrs. Jones. "We don't need a kid," he said. "He's just going to be baggage. We're going in on skis. There'll be blood. I can't waste one of my men holding his hand."

"I don't need to have my hand held," Alex retorted angrily. "She's right. I know more about Point Blanc than any of you. I've been there—and I got out of there, no thanks to you. Also, I've met some of those boys. One of them is a friend of mine. I promised I'd help him, and I will."

"Not if you get killed."

"I can look after myself!"

"Then it's agreed," Mrs. Jones said. "Alex will lead you in there, but then will take no further part in the operation. And as for his safety, Wolf, I will hold you personally responsible."

"Personally responsible. Right," Wolf growled.

Alex couldn't resist a smile. He'd held his ground, and he'd be going back in with the SAS. Then he realized what had happened. A few moments ago, he'd been arguing violently against doing just that. He glanced at the head of Special Operations. She'd manipulated him, of course, bringing Wolf into the room. And she knew it.

Wolf nodded. "All right, Cub," he said. "Looks like you're in. Let's go and play."

"Sure, Wolf," Alex sighed. "Let's go and play."

16

NIGHT RAID

THEY CAME SKIING DOWN from the mountain. There were seven of them, Wolf in front, Alex at his side. The other five men followed behind. They had changed into white trousers, jackets, and hoods—camouflage that would help them blend into the snow. A helicopter had dropped them two miles north and two hundred yards above Point Blanc, and equipped with night-vision goggles, they had quickly made their way down. The weather had settled again. The moon was out. Despite himself, Alex enjoyed the journey, the whisper of the skis cutting through the ice, the empty mountainside bathed in white light. And he was part of a crack SAS unit. He felt safe.

But then the academy loomed up below him, and once again he shivered. Before they had left, he had asked for a gun, but Wolf had shaken his head.

"I'm sorry, Cub. It's orders. You get us in, then you get out of sight."

It was the same old story. When they needed him, he was a man. When he asked to protect himself, he was just a kid.

There were no lights showing in the building. The helicopter had arrived back from Paris, crouching on the helipad like a glittering insect. The ski jump stood to one side, dark and forgotten. There was nobody in sight. Wolf held up a hand and they sliced to a halt.

"Guards?" he whispered.

"Two patrolling. One on the roof."

"Let's take him out first."

Mrs. Jones had made her instructions absolutely clear. There was to be no bloodshed unless absolutely necessary. The mission was to get the boys out. The SAS could take care of Dr. Grief, Mrs. Stellenbosch, and the guards at a later date.

Now Wolf held out a hand and one of the other men passed him something. It was a crossbow—not the medieval sort but a sophisticated, high-tech weapon with a microflite aluminium barrel and laser scope. He loaded it with an anesthetic dart, lifted it up, and took aim. Alex saw him smile to himself. Then his finger curled and the dart flashed across the night, traveling at three hundred feet per second. There was a faint sound from the roof of the academy. It was as if someone had coughed. Wolf lowered the crossbow.

"One down," he said.

"Sure," Alex muttered. "And about twenty-nine to go."

Wolf signaled and they continued down, more slowly now. They were about twenty yards from the school when they saw the main door open. Two men walked out, machine guns hanging from their shoulders. As one, the SAS men veered to the right, disappearing around the side of the school. They stopped within reach of the wall, dropping down to lie flat on their stomachs. Two of the men had moved slightly ahead. Alex noticed that they had kicked off their skis at the very same moment they had come to a halt.

The two guards approached. One of them was talking quietly in German. Alex's face was half buried in the snow. He knew the combat clothes would make him invisible. He half lifted his head just in time to see two figures rise out of the ground like ghosts from the grave. Two blackjacks swung in the moonlight. The guards crumpled. In seconds they were tied up and gagged. They wouldn't be going anywhere that night.

Wolf signaled again. The men got up and ran

forward, making for the main door. Alex hastily pulled his own skis off and followed. They reached the door in a line, their backs against the wall. Wolf looked inside to make sure it was safe. He nodded. They went in.

They were back in the hall with the stone dragons and the animal heads. Alex found himself next to Wolf and quickly gave him his bearings, pointing out the different rooms.

"The library?" Wolf whispered. He was totally serious now. Alex could see the tension in his eyes.

"Through here."

Wolf took a step forward, then crouched down, his hand whipping into one of the pouches of his jacket. Another guard had appeared, patrolling the lower corridor. Dr. Grief was taking no more chances. Wolf waited until the man had gone past and then nodded. One of the other SAS men went after him. Alex heard a thud and the soft clatter of a gun dropping.

"So far so good," Wolf whispered.

They went into the library. Alex showed Wolf how to summon the elevator, and Wolf whistled softly as the suit of armor smoothly divided into two parts. "This is quite a place," he muttered.

"Are you going up or down?"

"Down. Let's make sure the kids are all right."

There was just room for all seven of them in the elevator. Alex had warned Wolf about the guard at the table, in sight of the elevator, and Wolf took no chances: he came out firing. In fact, two guards were there. One of them was holding a mug of coffee while the other lit a cigarette. Wolf fired twice. Two more anesthetic darts traveled the short distance along the corridor and found their targets. Again, it had all happened in almost total silence. The two guards collapsed and lay still. The SAS men stepped out into the corridor.

Suddenly Alex remembered. He was angry with himself for not mentioning it before. "You can't go into the cells," he whispered. "They're wired up for sound."

Wolf nodded. "Show me!"

Alex showed Wolf the passage with the steel-lined doors. Wolf pointed to two of the men. "I want you to stay here. If we're found, this is the first place Grief will come."

The men nodded. They understood. The rest of them went back to the elevator, up to the library, and out into the hall.

Wolf turned to Alex. "We're going to have to

deactivate the system," he explained. "Do you have any idea . . . ?"

"This way. Grief's private rooms are on the other side."

But before he could finish, three more guards appeared, walking down the passageway. Wolf shot one of them—another anesthetic dart—and one of his men took out the other two. But this time they were a fraction of a second too slow. Alex saw one of the guards bring his gun around. He was probably unconscious before he managed to fire. But at the last moment, his finger tightened on the trigger. Bullets sprayed upward, smashing into the ceiling, bringing plaster and wood splinters showering down. Nobody had been hit, but the damage had been done. The lights flashed on. Once again, the alarm began to ring.

Twenty yards away, a door opened and more guards poured through.

"Down!" Wolf shouted.

He had produced a grenade. He tugged the pin out and threw it. Alex hit the ground, and a second later there was a soft explosion as a great cloud of tear gas filled the far end of the passage. The guards staggered, blind and helpless. The SAS men quickly took them out.

Wolf grabbed hold of him and dragged him close. "Find somewhere to hide!" he shouted. "You've got us in. We'll do the rest now."

"Give me a gun!" Alex shouted back. Some of the gas had reached him, and he could feel his eyes burning.

"No. I've got orders. At the first sign of trouble, you're to get out of the way. Find somewhere safe. We'll come for you later."

"Wolf!"

But Wolf was already up and running. Alex heard machine-gun fire coming from somewhere below. So Wolf had been right. One of the guards had been sent to take care of the prisoners—but there had been two SAS men waiting for him. And now the rules had changed. The SAS couldn't afford to risk the lives of the prisoners. There was going to be bloodshed. Alex could only imagine the battle that must be taking place. But he was to be no part of it. His job was to hide.

More explosions. More gunfire. There was a bitter taste in Alex's mouth as he made his way back to the stairs. It was typical of MI6. Half the time they would happily get him killed. The other half they treated him like a child. A guard appeared suddenly,

running toward the sound of the fighting. Alex's eyes
were still smarting from the gas, and now he made use
of it. He brought his hand up to his face, pretending
to cry. The guard saw a fourteen-year-old boy in
tears. He stopped. At that moment Alex twisted
around on his left foot, driving the upper part of his
right foot sideways into the man's stomach—the
roundhouse kick or *mawashi-geri* he had learned in
karate. The guard didn't even have time to cry out.
His eyes rolled and he went limp. Alex felt a little better after that.

But there was still nothing more for him to do.
There was another round of gunfire, then the quiet
blast of a second gas grenade. Alex went into the dining room. From here he could look out through the
windows at the side of the building and the helipad
above. He noticed that the blades of the helicopter
were turning. Somebody was inside it! He moved
closer to the window. It was Dr. Grief! He had to let
Wolf know.

He turned around.

Mrs. Stellenbosch was standing in front of him.

He had never seen her look less human. Her entire face was contorted with anger, her lips rolled outward, her eyes ablaze.

"You didn't die!" she exclaimed. "You're still alive!" Her voice was almost a whine, as if somehow none of it had been fair. "You brought them here. You've ruined everything!"

"That's what I'm paid for," Alex said.

"What was it that made me look in here?" Mrs. Stellenbosch giggled to herself. Alex could almost see the sanity slipping out of her. "Well, at least this is one bit of business I'm finally going to be able to finish."

Alex tensed himself, feet apart, gravity center low, just like he had been taught. But it was useless. Mrs. Stellenbosch lurched into him, moving with frightening speed. It was like being run over by a bus. Alex felt the full impact of her body weight, then cried out as two massive hands seized hold of him and threw him headfirst across the room. He crashed into a table, knocking it over, then rolled out of the way as Mrs. Stellenbosch followed up her first attack, lashing out with a kick that would have taken his head off his shoulders if it hadn't missed by less than an inch.

He scrambled to his feet and stood there, panting for breath. For a moment his vision was blurred. Blood trickled out of the corner of his mouth. Mrs. Stellenbosch charged again. Alex threw himself forward, using another of the tables for leverage. His feet swung around, scything through the air, both his heels catching her on the back of the head. Anyone else would have been knocked out by the blow. But although Alex felt the jolt of it running all the way up his body, Mrs. Stellenbosch hardly faltered. As Alex left the table, her hands swung down, smashing through the thick wood. The table fell apart and she walked through it, grabbing him again, this time by the neck. Alex felt his feet leave the floor. With a grunt she hurled him against the wall. Alex yelled, wondering if his back had been broken. He slid to the floor. He couldn't move.

Mrs. Stellenbosch stopped, breathing heavily. She glanced out the window. The helicopter's blades were at full speed now. The helicopter rocked forward then slowly rose into the air. It was time to go.

She reached down and picked up her handbag. She took out a gun and aimed at Alex. Alex stared at her. There was nothing he could do.

Mrs. Stellenbosch smiled. "And this is what *I* am paid for," she said.

The dining room door swung open.

"Alex!" It was Wolf. He was holding a machine gun.

Mrs. Stellenbosch lifted the gun up and fired three shots. Each one of them hit its target. Wolf was hit in the shoulder, the arm, and the chest. But even as he fell back, he opened fire himself. The heavy bullets slammed into Mrs. Stellenbosch. She was hurled backward into the window, which smashed behind her. With a scream she disappeared into the night and the snow, headfirst, her heavy, stockinged legs trailing behind.

The shock of what had happened gave Alex new strength. He got to his feet and ran over to Wolf. The SAS man wasn't dead, but he was badly hurt, his breath rattling.

"I'm okay," he managed to say. "Came looking for you. Glad I found you."

"Wolf . . ."

"Okay." He tapped at his chest and Alex saw that he was wearing body armor under his jacket. There was blood coming from his arm, but the other two bullets hadn't reached him. "Grief . . . ," he said.

Wolf gestured, and Alex looked around. The helicopter had left its launchpad. It was flying low outside the academy. Alex saw Dr. Grief in the pilot's seat. He had a gun. He fired. There was a yell, and a body fell from somewhere above. One of the SAS men.

Suddenly Alex was angry. Grief was a freak, a monster. He was responsible for all this—and he was going to get away. Not knowing what he was doing, he snatched up Wolf's gun and ran through the broken window, past the dead body of Mrs. Stellenbosch and into the night. He tried to aim. The blades of the helicopter were whipping up the surface snow, blinding him, but he pointed the gun up and fired. Nothing happened. He pulled the trigger again. Still nothing. Either Wolf had used all his ammunition or the gun had jammed.

Dr. Grief pulled at the controls and the helicopter banked away, following the slope of the mountain. It was too late. Nothing could stop him.

Unless . . .

Alex threw down the gun and ran forward. There was a snowmobile lying idle a few yards away, its engine still running. The man who had been riding it was lying facedown in the snow. Alex leapt onto the seat and turned the throttle full on. The snowmobile roared away, skimming over the ice, following the path of the helicopter.

Dr. Grief saw him. The helicopter slowed and turned. Grief raised a hand, waving good-bye. Alex caught sight of the red glasses, the slender fingers raised in one last gesture of defiance. With his hands gripping the handlebars, Alex stood up on the foot grips, tensing himself for what he knew he had to do. The helicopter moved away again, gaining altitude. In front of Alex loomed the ski jump. He was traveling at seventy, eighty miles per hour, snow and wind rushing past him. Ahead of him there was a wooden barrier, shaped like a cross.

Alex smashed through it, then threw himself off.

The snowmobile plunged down, its engine screaming.

Alex rolled over and over in the snow, ice and wood splinters in his eyes and mouth. He managed to get to his knees.

The snowmobile reached the end of the ski jump.

Alex watched it rocket into the air, propelled by the huge metal slide.

In the helicopter, Dr. Grief just had time to see five hundred pounds of solid steel come hurtling toward him out of the night, its headlights blazing, its engine still screaming. His eyes, bright red, opened wide in shock. The makeshift torpedo hit its target full-on. Point-blank.

The explosion lit up the entire mountain. The helicopter disappeared in a huge fireball, then plunged down. It was still burning when it hit the ground.

Behind him, Alex became aware that the shooting had stopped. The battle was over. He walked slowly back to the academy, shivering suddenly in the cold night air. As he approached, a man appeared at the broken window and waved. It was Wolf, propping himself against the wall, but still very much alive. Alex went over to him.

"What happened to Grief?" he asked.

"It looks like I 'sleighed' him," Alex replied.

On the slopes, the wreckage of the helicopter flickered and burned as the morning sun began to rise.

17

DEAD RINGER

A FEW DAYS LATER, ALEX found himself sitting opposite Alan Blunt in the faceless office on Liverpool Street, with Mrs. Jones twisting another peppermint between her fingers. It was May 1, a bank holiday in England, but somehow he knew that holidays never came to the building that called itself the Royal & General Bank. Even the spring seemed to have stopped at the window. Outside, the sun was shining. Inside, there were only shadows.

"It seems that once again we owe you a debt of thanks," Blunt was saying.

"You don't owe me anything," Alex said.

Blunt looked genuinely puzzled. "You have quite possibly changed the future of this planet," he said. "Of course, Grief's plan was monstrous, crazy. But the fact remains that his . . ." He searched for a word to describe the test-tube creations that had been sent out of Point Blanc. ". . . his offspring could have caused a great many problems. At the very least they would have had money. God knows what they would have done had they remained undiscovered."

"What's happened to them?" Alex asked.

"We've traced all fifteen of them, and we have them under lock and key," Mrs. Jones answered. "They were quietly arrested by the intelligence services of each country where they lived. We'll take care of them."

Alex shivered. He had a feeling he knew what Mrs. Jones had meant by those last words. And he was certain that nobody would ever see the fifteen Grief replicas again.

"Once again, we've had to hush this up," Blunt continued. "This whole business of . . . cloning. It causes a great deal of public disquiet. Sheep are one thing—but human beings!" He coughed. "The families involved in this business have no desire for publicity, so they won't be talking. They're just glad to have had their real sons returned to them. The same, of course, goes for you, Alex. You've already signed the Official Secrets Act. I'm sure we can trust you to be discreet."

There was a moment's pause. Mrs. Jones looked carefully at Alex. She had to admit that she was worried about him. She knew everything that had happened at Point Blanc, how close he had come to a horrible death, only to be sent back into the academy for a second time. The boy who had come back from the French Alps was different from the one who had left. There was a coldness about him, as tangible as the mountain snow.

"You did very well, Alex," she said.

"How is Wolf?" Alex asked.

"He's fine. He's still in the hospital, but the doctors say he'll make a complete recovery. We hope to have him back on operations in a few weeks."

"That's good."

"We had only one fatality in the raid on Point Blanc. That was the man you saw falling from the roof. Wolf and another man were injured. Otherwise, it was a complete success." She paused. "Is there anything else you want to know?"

"No." Alex shook his head. He stood up. "You left me in there," he said. "I called for help and you didn't come. Grief was going to kill me, but you didn't care."

"That's not true, Alex." Mrs. Jones glanced at

Blunt for support, but he didn't meet her eyes. "There were difficulties . . ."

"It doesn't matter. I just want you to know that I've had enough. I don't want to be a spy anymore, and if you ask me again, I'll refuse. I know you think you can blackmail me. But I know too much about you now, so that won't work anymore." He walked over to the door. "I used to think that being a spy would be exciting and special, like in the films. But you just used me. In a way, the two of you are as bad as Grief. You'll do anything to get what you want. Well, I want to go back to school. Next time, you can do it without me."

There was a long silence after Alex had left. At last Blunt spoke. "He'll be back," he said.

Mrs. Jones raised an eyebrow. "You really think so?"

"He's too good at what he does—too good at the job. And it's in his blood." He stood up. "It's rather odd," he said. "Most schoolboys dream of being a spy. With Alex, we have a spy who dreams of being a schoolboy."

"Will you really use him again?" Mrs. Jones asked.

"Of course. There was a file that came in only this morning. An interesting case. Right up his alley." He smiled. "We'll give him a few days to settle down and then we'll call him."

"He won't answer."

"We'll see," Blunt said.

Alex walked home from the bus stop and let himself into the elegant Chelsea house that he shared with his housekeeper and closest friend, Jack Starbright. Jack knew where Alex had been and what he had been doing. But the two of them had made an agreement never to discuss his involvement with MI6. She didn't like it, and she worried about him. But ultimately, they both knew, there was nothing more to be said.

She seemed surprised to see him. "I thought you'd just gone out," she said.

"No."

"Did you get the message by the phone?"

"What message?"

"Mr. Bray wants to see you this afternoon. Three o'clock at the school."

Henry Bray was the principal at Brookland. Alex wasn't surprised by the summons. Bray was the sort of principal who managed to run a busy school and still find time to take a personal interest in every pupil there. He had been worried by Alex's long absence at

the start of spring term. The fact that Alex had also
missed the last two weeks of the same term had worried him more. So he had called a meeting.

"Do you want lunch?" Jack asked.

"No, thanks." Alex knew that he would have to
pretend he had been ill again. Doubtless MI6 would
produce another doctor's note in due course. But the
thought of lying to his principal had spoiled his appetite.

He set off an hour later, taking his bicycle, which
had been returned to the house by the Putney police.
He cycled slowly. It was good to be back in London,
to be surrounded by normal life. He turned off the
King's Road and pedaled down the side road where—
it felt like a month ago—he had followed the man in
the white Skoda. The school loomed up ahead of him.
It was empty now and would remain so until the summer term.

But as Alex arrived, he saw a figure walking across
the yard to the school gates and recognized Mr. Lee,
the elderly school caretaker.

"You again!"

"Hello, Bernie," Alex said. That was what everyone called him.

"On your way to see Mr. Bray?"

"Yeah."

The caretaker shook his head. "He never told me he was going to be here today. But he never tells me anything! I'm just going down to the shops. I'll be back at five to lock up, so make sure you're out by then."

"Right, Bernie."

There was nobody in the school yard. It felt strange, walking across the tarmac on his own. The school seemed bigger with nobody there, the yard stretching out too far between the redbrick buildings with the sun beating down, reflecting off the windows. Alex was dazzled. He had never seen the place so empty and so quiet. The grass on the playing fields looked almost too green. Any school without schoolchildren has its own peculiar atmosphere, and Brookland was no exception.

Mr. Bray had an office in D block, which was next to the science building. Alex reached the swinging doors and opened them. The walls here would normally be covered in posters, but they had all been taken down at the end of the term. Everything was blank, off-white. There was another door open to one side. Bernie had been cleaning the main laboratory. He had rested his mop and bucket to one side when he had gone to the shops—to pick up cigarettes, Alex presumed. The man had been a chain smoker all his life, and Alex knew he'd die with a cigarette between his lips.

Alex climbed up the stairs, his heels rapping against the stone surface. He reached a corridor—left for biology, right for physics—and continued straight ahead. A second corridor, with full-length windows on both sides, led into D block. Bray's study was directly ahead of him. He stopped at the door, vaguely wondering if he should have dressed up for the meeting. Bray was always snapping at boys with their shirts hanging out or crooked ties. Alex was wearing a Gortex jacket, T-shirt, jeans, and Nike sneakers—the same clothes he had worn that morning at MI6. His hair was still too short for his liking, although it had begun to grow back. All in all, he still looked like a juvenile delinquent—but it was too late now. And anyway, Bray didn't want to see him to discuss his appearance. His nonappearance at school was more to the point.

He knocked on the door.

"Come in!" a voice called.

Alex opened the door and walked into the principal's study, a cluttered room with views over the

school yard. There was a desk, piled high with pa-
pers, and a black leather chair with its back toward
the door. A cabinet full of trophies stood against one
wall. The others were mainly lined with books.

"You wanted to see me," Alex said.

The chair turned slowly around.

Alex froze.

It wasn't Henry Bray sitting behind the desk.

It was himself.

He was looking at a fourteen-year-old boy with
fair hair cut very short, brown eyes, and a slim, pale
face. The boy was even dressed identically to him. It
took Alex what felt like an eternity to accept what he
was seeing. He was standing in a room looking at
himself sitting in a chair. The boy *was* him.

With just one difference. The boy was holding a
gun.

"Come in," he said.

Alex didn't move. He knew what he was facing
and he was angry with himself for not having expected
it. When he had been handcuffed at the academy, Dr.
Grief had boasted to him that he had cloned himself
sixteen times. But that morning Mrs. Jones had traced
"all fifteen of them." That left one spare—one boy
waiting to take his place in the family of Sir David

Friend. Alex had glimpsed him while he was at the academy. Now he remembered the figure with the white mask, watching him from a window as he walked over to the ski jump. The white mask had been bandages. The new Alex had been spying on him as he recovered from the plastic surgery that had made the two of them identical.

And even today there had been clues. Perhaps it had been the heat of the sun, or the fallout from his visit to MI6. But he had been too wrapped up in his own thoughts to see them.

Jack, when he got home. *"I thought you'd just gone out."*

Bernie, at the gate. *"You again!"*

They had both thought they'd seen him. And in a sense, they had. They had seen the boy sitting opposite him. The boy who was now aiming a gun at his heart.

"I've been looking forward to this," the other boy said, and despite the hatred in his voice, Alex couldn't help marveling. The voice wasn't the same as his. The boy hadn't had enough time to get it right. But otherwise he was a dead ringer.

"What are you doing here?" Alex said. "It's all

over. The Gemini Project is finished. You might as well turn yourself in. You need help."

"I need just one thing," the second Alex sneered. "I need to see you dead. I'm going to shoot you. I'm going to do it now. You killed my father!"

"Your father was a test tube," Alex said. "You never had a mother or a father. You're a freak. Handmade in the French Alps, like a cuckoo clock. What are you going to do when you've killed me? Take my place? You wouldn't last a week. You may look like me, but too many people know what Grief was trying to do. And I'm sorry, but you've got 'fake' written all over you."

"We would have had everything! We would have had the whole world!" The replica Alex almost screamed the words, and for a moment Alex thought he heard Dr. Grief somewhere in there, blaming him from beyond the grave. But then the creature in front of him *was* Dr. Grief . . . or part of him. "I don't care what happens to me," he went on, "just so long as you're dead."

The hand with the gun stretched out. The barrel was pointing at him. Alex looked the boy straight in the eyes.

And he saw the hesitation.

The fake Alex couldn't quite bring himself to do it. They were too similar. The same clothes, the same bodies, the same faces. For the other boy, it would be like shooting himself. Alex still hadn't closed the door. He threw himself backward, out into the corridor. At the same time, the gun went off, the bullet exploding inches above his head and crashing into the far wall. Alex hit the ground on his back and rolled out of the doorway as a second bullet slammed into the floor. And then he was running, putting as much space between himself and his double as he could.

There was a third shot as he sprinted down the corridor, and the window next to him shattered, glass showering down. Alex reached the stairs and took them three at a time, afraid that he would trip and break an ankle. But then he was at the bottom, heading for the main door, swerving only when he realized that he would make too easy a target as he crossed the school yard. Instead he dived into the laboratory, almost falling headfirst over Bernie's bucket and mop.

The laboratory was long and rectangular, divided into workstations with Bunsen burners, flasks, and dozens of bottles of chemicals spread out on shelves that stretched the full length of the room. There was another door at the far end. Alex dived behind the farthest desk. Would his double have seen him come in? Might he be looking for him, even now, out in the yard?

Cautiously, Alex poked his head over the surface, then ducked down as four bullets ricocheted around him, splintering the wood and smashing one of the gas pipes. Alex heard the hiss of escaping gas. Then there was another gunshot and an explosion that hurled him backward, sprawling onto the floor. The last bullet had ignited the gas. Flames leapt up, licking at the ceiling. At the same time, the sprinkler system went off, spraying the entire room. Alex tracked back on his hands and feet, searching for shelter behind fire and water, hoping the other Alex would be blinded. His shoulders hit the far door. He scrambled to his feet. There was another shot. But then he was through—with another corridor and a second flight of stairs straight ahead.

The stairs led nowhere. He was halfway up before he remembered. There was a single classroom at the top that was used for biology. It had a spiral staircase leading to the roof. The school had so little land that they'd planned to build a roof garden. Then they'd run out of money. There were a couple of greenhouses. Nothing more.

There was no way down! Alex looked over his shoulder and saw the other Alex reloading his gun, already on his way up. He had no choice. He had to continue even though he would soon be trapped.

He reached the biology classroom and slammed the door shut behind him. There was no lock, and the tables were all bolted into the floor. Otherwise he might be able to make a barricade. The spiral staircase was ahead of him. He ran up it without stopping, through another door and onto the roof. Alex stopped to catch his breath and see what he could do next.

He was standing on a wide, flat area with a fence running all the way around. There were half a dozen terra-cotta pots filled with earth. A few plants sprouted out, looking more dead than alive. Alex sniffed the air. Smoke was curling up from the windows two floors below, and he realized that the sprinkler system had been unable to put out the fire. He thought of the gas, pouring into the room, and the chemicals stacked up on the shelves. He could be standing on a time bomb! He had to find a way down.

But then he heard the sound of feet on metal and realized that his double had reached the top of the spiral staircase. Alex ducked behind one of the greenhouses. The door crashed open.

Smoke followed the fake Alex out onto the roof. He took a step forward. Now Alex was behind him.

"Where are you?" the fake Alex shouted. His hair was soaked and his face contorted with anger.

Alex knew his moment had come. He would never have a better chance. He ran forward. The other Alex twisted around and fired. The bullet creased his shoulder, a molten sword drawn across his flesh. But a second later he had reached him, grabbing him around the neck with one hand and seizing hold of his wrist with the other, forcing the gun away. There was a huge explosion in the laboratory below and the entire building shook, but neither of the boys seemed to notice. They were locked in an embrace, two reflections that had become tangled up in the mirror, the gun over their heads, fighting for control.

The flames were tearing through the building. Fed by a variety of chemicals, they burst through the floor, melting the asphalt. In the far distance, the scream of fire engines penetrated the sun-filled air. Alex pulled with all his strength, trying to bring the gun down. The other Alex clawed at him, swearing—not in English but in Afrikaans.

The end came very suddenly.

The gun twisted and fell to the ground.

One Alex lashed out, knocking the other one down, then dived for the gun.

There was another explosion, and a sheet of chemical flame leapt up. A crater had suddenly appeared in the roof, swallowing up the gun. The boy saw it too late and fell through. With a yell, he disappeared into the smoke and fire.

One Alex Rider walked over to the hole and looked down.

The other Alex Rider lay on his back, two floors below. He wasn't moving. The flames were closing in.

The first fire engines had arrived at the school. A ladder slanted up toward the roof.

A boy with short fair hair and brown eyes, wearing a Gortex jacket, T-shirt, and jeans, walked to the edge of the roof and began to climb down.

*Turn the page for a preview
of the next Alex Rider Adventure,*

SKELETON KEY

1
IN THE DARK

NIGHT CAME QUICKLY to Skeleton Key.

The sun hovered briefly on the horizon, then dipped below. At once, the clouds rolled in—first red, then mauve, silver, green, and black, as though all the colors in the world were being sucked into a vast melting pot. A single frigatebird soared over the mangroves, its own colors lost in the chaos behind it. The air was close. Rain hung waiting. There was going to be a storm.

The single-engine Cessna Skyhawk SP circled twice before coming in to land. It was the sort of plane that would barely have been noticed, flying in this part of the world. That was why it had been chosen. If anyone had been curious enough to check the registration number, printed under the wing, they would have learned that this plane belonged to a photographic company based in Jamaica. This was not true. There was no company, and it was already too dark to take photographs. But nothing had been left to chance.

There were three men in the aircraft. They were all dark-skinned, wearing faded jeans and loose, open-neck shirts. The pilot had long, black hair, deep brown eyes, and a thin scar running down the side of his face. He had met his two passengers only that afternoon. They had introduced themselves as Carlo and Marc, but he doubted that these were their real names. He knew their journey had begun a long time ago, somewhere in Eastern Europe. He knew this short flight was the last leg. He knew what they were carrying. Already, he knew too much.

He glanced down at the multifunction display in the control board. The illuminated computer screen was warning him about the storm that was closing in. That didn't worry the pilot. Low clouds and rain gave him cover. The authorities were less vigilant during a storm. Even so, he was nervous. He had flown in to Cuba many times. But never here. And tonight he would have preferred to have been going almost anywhere else.

Cayo Esqueleto. Skeleton Key.

There it was, stretching out before him, twenty-five miles long and six miles across at its widest point.

The sea around it, which had been an extraordinary, brilliant blue until a few minutes ago, had suddenly darkened, as if someone had thrown a switch. Over to the west, he made out the twinkling lights of Puerto Madre, the island's second-biggest town. The main airport was farther north, outside the capital of Santiago. But that wasn't where he was heading. He pressed down on the joystick and the plane veered to the right, circling over the forests and mangrove swamps that surrounded the old, abandoned airport at the bottom end of the island.

The Cessna had been equipped with a thermal intensifier, similar to the sort used in American spy satellites. He flicked a switch and glanced at the display. A few birds appeared as tiny pinpricks of red. More dots pulsated in the swamp: crocodiles or perhaps manatees. And a single dot about twenty yards from the runway. He turned to speak to the man called Carlo, but there was no need. Carlo was already leaning over his shoulder, staring at the screen.

Carlo nodded. Only one man was waiting for them, as agreed. Anyone hiding within half a mile of the airstrip would have shown up on the radar. It was safe to land.

The pilot looked out the window. The runway was

a rough strip of land on the edge of the coast, hacked out of the jungle and running parallel with the sea. The pilot could have missed it altogether in the dying light but for the two lines of electric bulbs burning at ground level, outlining the path for the plane.

The Cessna swooped out of the sky. At the last minute it was buffeted about by a sudden, damp squall that had been sent to try the pilot's nerve. But the pilot didn't blink, and a moment later the wheels hit the ground and the plane was bouncing and shuddering along, dead center between the two rows of lights. He was grateful they were there. The mangroves—thick bushes, half floating on pools of stagnant water—came almost to the edge of the runway. Veer even a couple of yards in the wrong direction and a wheel might snag. It would be enough to destroy the plane.

The pilot flicked switches. The engine died and the twin-blade propellers slowed down and came to a halt. He looked out the window. A Jeep was parked next to one of the buildings, and it was here that the single man—the red dot on his screen—waited. He turned to his passengers.

"He's there."

The older of the two men nodded. Carlo was about thirty years old with black, curly hair. He hadn't shaved. Stubble the color of cigarette ash clung to his jaw. He turned to the other passenger. "Marc? Are you ready?"

The man who called himself Marc could have been Carlo's younger brother. He was barely twenty-five, and although he was trying not to show it, he was scared. There was sweat on the side of his face, glowing green as it caught the reflection from the control panel. He reached behind him and took out a gun, a German-built 10mm Glock Automatic. He made sure it was loaded, then slipped it into the waistband of his trousers, under his shirt.

"I'm ready," he said.

"There is only him. There are two of us," Carlo tried to reassure Marc. Or perhaps he was trying to reassure himself. "We're both armed. There is nothing he can do."

"Then let's go."

Carlo turned to the pilot. "Have the plane ready," he commanded. "When we walk back, I will give you a sign." He raised a hand, one finger and thumb forming an *O*. "That is the signal that the business has been successfully concluded. Start the engine at that time. We don't want to stay here one second longer than we have to."

They got out of the plane. A thin layer of sand crunched underneath their combat boots as they walked around the side and opened the cargo door. They felt the sullen heat in the air, the heaviness of the night sky. The island seemed to be holding its breath. Carlo reached up and opened a door. In the back of the plane was a single steel chest. With difficulty, he and Marc lowered it to the ground.

The younger man looked up. The lights on the landing strip dazzled him, but he could just make out a figure standing, still as a statue, beside the Jeep, waiting for them to approach. He hadn't moved since the plane had landed. "Why doesn't he come to us?" he asked.

Carlo spat and said nothing.

There were two handles, one on either side of the chest. The two men carried it between them, walking awkwardly, bending over their load. It took them a long time to reach the Jeep. But at last they were there. For a second time, they set the box down.

Carlo straightened up, rubbing his palms on his jeans. "Good evening, General," he said. He was speaking in English. This was not his native language. Nor was it the general's. But it was the only language they had in common.

"Good evening." The general did not bother with names that he knew would be fake anyway. "You had no trouble getting here?"

"No trouble at all, General."

"You have it?"

"One kilogram of weapons-grade uranium. Enough to build a bomb powerful enough to destroy a city. I would be interested to know which city you have in mind."

General Alexei Sarov took a step forward and the lights from the runway illuminated him. He was not a big man, yet he radiated power and control. He still carried with him his years in the army. They could be seen in his close-cut, iron gray hair, his watchful, pale blue eyes, his almost emotionless face. They were in the very way he carried himself. He was perfectly poised, relaxed and wary at the same time. General Sarov was sixty-two years old but looked twenty years younger. He was dressed in a dark suit, a white shirt, and a narrow, dark blue tie. In the damp heat of the evening, his clothes should have been creased. He should have been sweating. But to look at him, he could have just stepped out of an air-conditioned room.

He crouched down beside the box, at the same time producing a small device from his pocket. It looked like a car cigarette lighter with a dial attached. He found a socket in the side of the metal crate and plugged in the device. Briefly, he examined the dial. He nodded. It was satisfactory.

"You have the rest of the money?" Carlo asked.

"Of course." The general straightened up and walked over to the Jeep. Carlo and Marc tensed themselves, for this was the moment when he might produce a gun. But when he turned around he was holding a black leather attaché case. He flicked the locks and opened it. The case was filled with banknotes: one-hundred-dollar bills neatly banded together in packets of fifty. One hundred packets in all. A total of half a million dollars. More money than Carlo had ever seen in his life.

But still not enough.

"We've had a problem," Carlo said.

"Yes?" Sarov did not sound surprised.

Marc could feel the sweat as it drew a comma down the side of his neck. A mosquito was whining in his ear but he resisted the urge to slap it. This was what he had been waiting for. He was standing a few steps away, his hands hanging limply by his sides. Slowly, he allowed them to creep behind him, closer to the concealed gun. He glanced at the ruined buildings. One might once have been a control tower. The other looked like a customs shed. Both of them were broken and empty, the brickwork crumbling, the windows smashed. Could there be someone hiding there? No. The thermal intensifier would have shown them. They were alone.

"The cost of the uranium." Carlo shrugged. "Our friend in Miami sends his apologies. But there are new security systems all over the world. Smuggling . . . particularly this sort of thing . . . has become much more difficult. And that's meant extra expense."

"How much extra expense?"

"A quarter of a million dollars."

"That's unfortunate."

"Unfortunate for you, General. You're the one who must pay."

Sarov considered. "We had an agreement," he said.

"Our friend in Miami hoped you'd understand."

There was a long silence. Marc's fingers reached out behind his back, closing around the Glock

Automatic. But then Sarov nodded. "I will have to raise the money," he said.

"You can have it transferred to the same account that we used before," Carlo said. "But I have to warn you, General. If the money hasn't arrived in three days, the American intelligence services will be told what has happened here tonight . . . what you've just received. You may think you are safe here on this island. I can assure you, you won't be safe anymore."

"You're threatening me," Sarov muttered, and there was something at once calm and deadly in the way he spoke.

"It's nothing personal," Carlo said.

Quickly, Marc produced a cloth bag. He unfolded it, then tipped the money out of the case and into the bag. The case might contain a radio transmitter. It might contain a small bomb. He left it behind.

"Good night, General," Carlo said.

"Good night." Sarov smiled. "I hope you enjoy the flight."

The two men walked away. Marc could feel the money, the bundles pressing through the cloth against the side of his leg. "The man's a fool," he whispered, returning to his own language. "An old man. Why were we afraid?"

"Let's just get out of here," Carlo said. He was thinking about what the general had said. *I hope you enjoy the flight*. Had he been smiling when he said that?

He made the agreed-upon signal, pressing his finger and thumb together. At once the Cessna's engine started up.

General Sarov was still watching them. He hadn't moved, but now his hand reached once again into his jacket pocket. His fingers closed around the radio transmitter waiting there. He had wondered if it would be necessary to kill the two men and their pilot. Personally, he would have preferred not to, even as an insurance policy. But their demands had made it necessary. He should have known they would be greedy. Given the sort of people they were, it was almost inevitable.

Back in the plane, the two men were strapping themselves into their seats while the pilot prepared for takeoff. Carlo heard the engine rev up as the plane began slowly to turn. Far away, there was a low rumble of thunder. Now he wished that they had turned the plane around immediately after they had landed. It would have saved some precious seconds and he was eager to be away, back in the air.

I hope you enjoy the flight.

There had been no emotion whatsoever in the general's voice. He could have meant what he was saying. But Carlo guessed he would have spoken exactly the same way if he had been passing a sentence of death.

Next to him, Marc was already counting the money, running his hands through the piles of bills. He looked back at the ruined buildings, at the waiting Jeep. Would Sarov try something? What sort of resources did he have on the island? But as the plane turned in a tight circle, nothing moved. The general stayed where he was. There was nobody else in sight.

Then the runway lights went out.

"What the? . . ." The pilot swore viciously.

Marc stopped his counting. Carlo understood at once what had happened. "He's turned the lights off," he said. "He wants to keep us here. Can you take off without them?"

The plane had turned a half circle so that it was facing the way it had come. The pilot stared out the cockpit window, straining to see into the night. It was very dark now, but there was an ugly, unnatural light pulsating in the sky. He nodded. "It won't be easy . . ."

The lights came back on again.

There they were, stretching into the distance, an arrow that pointed to freedom and an extra profit of a quarter of a million dollars. The pilot relaxed. "It must have been the storm," he said. "It disrupted the electricity supply."

"Just get us out of here," Carlo muttered. "The sooner we're in the air, the happier I'll be."

The pilot nodded. "Whatever you say." He pressed down with the controls and the Cessna lumbered forward, picking up speed quickly. The runway lights blurred, guiding him forward. Carlo settled back into his seat. Marc was still watching out of the window.

And then, seconds before the wheels left the ground, the plane suddenly lurched. The whole world twisted as a giant, invisible hand seized hold of it and wrenched it sideways. The Cessna had been traveling at 120 miles per hour. It came to a grinding halt in a matter of seconds, the deceleration throwing all three men forward in their seats. If they hadn't been belted in, they would have been hurled out the front window—or what was left of the shattered glass. At the same time there was a series of ear-shattering crashes as something whipped into the fuselage. One of the wings had dipped down and the propeller was torn off, spinning into the night. Suddenly the plane was still, resting, tilted, on one side.

For a moment, nobody inside the cabin moved. The plane's engines rattled and stopped. Then Marc pulled himself up in his seat. "What happened?" he screamed. "What happened?" He had bitten his tongue. Blood trickled down his chin. The bag was still open and money had spilled into his lap.

"I don't understand . . ." The pilot was too dazed to speak.

"You left the runway!" Carlo's face was twisted with anger.

"I didn't!"

"There!" Marc was pointing at something and Carlo followed his quivering finger. The door on the underside of the plane had buckled. Black water was seeping in underneath, forming a pool around their feet.

There was another rumble of thunder, closer this time.

"He did this!" the pilot said.

"What did he do?" Carlo demanded.

"He moved the runway!"

It had been a simple trick. As the plane had turned, Sarov had turned the lights off on the runway, using the radio transmitter in his pocket. For a moment, the pilot had been disoriented, lost in the darkness. Then the plane had finished its turn and the lights had come back on. But what the pilot hadn't known, what he wouldn't have been able to see, was that it was a second set of lights that had been activated—and that these had run off at an angle, leaving the safety of the runway and continuing over the surface of the swamp.

"He led us into the mangroves," the pilot said.

Now Carlo understood what had happened to the plane. The moment its wheels had touched the water, its fate had been sealed. Without solid ground underneath them, they had become bogged down and had toppled over. Swamp water was even now pouring in as they slowly sank beneath the surface. The branches of the mangrove trees that had almost torn the plane apart now surrounded them, bars of a living prison.

"What are we going to do?" Marc demanded, and suddenly he was sounding like a child. "We're going to drown!"

"We can get out!" Carlo had suffered whiplash injuries in the collision. He moved one arm painfully, unfastening his seat belt.

"We shouldn't have tried to cheat him!" Marc cried. "You knew what he was. You were told—"

"Shut up!" Carlo had a gun of his own. He pulled it out of the holster underneath his shirt and balanced it on his knee. "We'll get out of here and we'll kill him. And then somehow we'll find a way off this damn island."

"There's something out there," the pilot said.

Something had moved outside.

"What is it?" Marc whispered.

"Sssh!" Carlo half stood up, his body filling the cramped space of the cabin. The plane tilted again, settling farther into the swamp. He lost his balance, then steadied himself. He reached out, past the pilot, as though he was going to climb out the broken front window.

Something huge and horrible lunged toward him, blocking out what little light there was in the night sky. Carlo screamed as it threw itself head-first into the plane and onto him. There was a glint of white and a dreadful grunting sound. The other men were screaming now too.

General Sarov stood watching. It wasn't raining yet, but the water was heavy in the air. A sudden flash of lightning crossed the sky in slow motion, relishing its journey. In that moment, he saw the Cessna half buried on its side in the swamp. There were now half a dozen crocodiles swarming all over it. The largest of them had dived headfirst into the cockpit. Only its tail was visible, thrashing about as it gorged itself.

He reached down and lifted up the lead chest. Although it had taken two men to carry it to him, it seemed to weigh nothing in his hands. He placed it in the Jeep, then stood back. He allowed himself the rare privilege of a smile and he felt it, briefly, on his lips. Tomorrow, when the crocodiles had finished their meal, he would send his fieldworkers—the *macheteros*—in to recover the banknotes. Not that the money was important. He was the owner of a kilogram of weapons-grade uranium. As Carlo had said, he now had the power to destroy a small city.

But Sarov had no intention of destroying a city.

His target was the entire world.